ARMANCE
BY
Stendhal

ARMANCE

Published by Yurita Press

New York City, NY

First published 1827

Copyright © Yurita Press, 2015

All rights reserved

ABOUT KRILL PRESS

Krill Press is a boutique publishing company run by people who are passionate about history's greatest works. We strive to republish the best books ever written across every conceivable genre and making them easily and cheaply available to readers across the world. Please visit our site for more information.

FOREWORD

Armance is the first novel written by the French author Stendhal. The book is set during the Bourbon Restoration. A table of contents is included.

Armance

CHAPTER ONE

It is old and plain ...
It is silly sooth
And dallies with the
innocence of love.
    TWELFTH NIGHT, Act II.

On his twentieth birthday, Octave had just left the École
Polytechnique. His father, the Marquis de Malivert, wished to keep his
only son in Paris. As soon as Octave understood that this was the
constant desire of a father whom he respected, and of his mother whom
he loved with an almost passionate love, he abandoned his intention of
entering the Artillery. He would have liked to spend a few years in a
regiment, and then resign his commission until the next war, in which
he was equally ready to serve as Lieutenant or with the rank of
Colonel. This is typical of the eccentricities which made him odious
to the common run of humanity.

Plenty of brains, a tall figure, refined manners, the handsomest great
dark eyes in the world, would have assured Octave a place among the
most distinguished young men in society, had not a certain sombre air,
imprinted in those gentle eyes, led people to pity rather than to envy
him. He would have created a sensation had he been in the habit of
talking; but Octave desired nothing, nothing appeared to cause him
either pain or pleasure. Frequently ill in his childhood, ever since
vital energy had assumed control of his organism he had always been
observed to submit without hesitation to what seemed to him to be
prescribed by duty; but it might have been thought that, if Duty had
not made her voice heard, he would not have had, in himself,
sufficient impulse to make him act. Perhaps some singular principle,
deeply impressed upon his youthful heart, and incompatible with the
events of real life, as he saw them develop round about him, led him
to portray to himself in too sombre colours both his own future and
his relations with his fellow men. Whatever the cause of his profound
melancholy, Octave seemed to have turned misanthrope before his time.
Commander de Soubirane, his uncle, said one day in his presence that
the boy's nature alarmed him. "Why should I appear other than what I
am?" was Octave's cold reply. "Your nephew will always keep to the
line of reason." "But never rise above or fall below it," retorted the
Commander with his Provençal vivacity; "from which I conclude that if
you are not the Messiah expected by the Hebrews, you are Lucifer in

person, come back to this world on purpose to worry me. What the devil are you? I can't make you out; you are duty _incarnate_." "How happy I should be never to fail in my duty!" said Octave; "how I wish I could render up my soul pure to my Creator, as I received it from Him!" "A miracle!" exclaimed the Commander; "in the last twelvemonth, this is the first wish I have seen spring from a heart frozen stiff with purity." And in order not to spoil the effect of this utterance, the Commander hastily left the room.

Octave looked tenderly at his mother; she knew whether his heart was indeed frozen. It might be said of Madame de Malivert that she had remained young although approaching her fiftieth birthday. It was not only that she was still beautiful; she had, together with an exceptionally sharp intellect, retained a keen and active sympathy with her friends' interests, including the joys and sorrows of young men. She entered naturally into their reasons for hope or fear; and soon seemed to be hoping or fearing herself. This kind of character has lost its charm now that public opinion seems to have made it almost obligatory upon women of a certain age who are not religious; but there was never the least trace of affectation in Madame de Malivert.

Her servants had observed for some time past that she was in the habit of driving out in a hackney carriage; and often, when she came home, she was not alone. Saint-Jean, an inquisitive old footman, who had accompanied his employers during the emigration, tried to discover who a certain man was whom Madame de Malivert had more than once brought home with her. On the first occasion, Saint-Jean lost sight of the stranger in the crowd; at his second attempt, his curiosity was more successful; he saw the person whom he was following pass into the Charity Hospital, where he learned from the porter that the stranger was none other than the famous Doctor Duquerrel. Madame de Malivert's household discovered that their mistress was bringing to the house in turn all the most eminent doctors in Paris, and almost always she found an excuse for letting them see her son.

Struck by the eccentricities which she remarked in Octave, she feared lest his lungs might be affected; but she believed that, were she unfortunately to have been right in her diagnosis, naming that cruel malady would be tantamount to hastening its advance. Doctors, who were men of intelligence, assured Madame de Malivert that her son was suffering from no malady beyond that sort of dissatisfied and critical melancholy characteristic of the young men of his generation and position; but they warned her that she herself ought to pay the closest attention to her lungs. These dread tidings were divulged to the household by a régime which had to be enforced; and M. de Malivert, from whom a vain attempt was made to conceal the name of the malady, foresaw the possibility of being left alone in his old age. Extremely rich and extravagant before the Revolution, the Marquis de Malivert, who had not set foot again in France until 1814, in the train of his monarch, found himself reduced by the confiscations to an income of twenty or thirty thousand livres. He thought himself a beggar. The sole occupation of a mind that had never been any too powerful was now to seek a bride for Octave. But, being still more faithful to his code of honour than to the obsession that was tormenting him, the old Marquis de Malivert never failed to begin the overtures that he made in society with these words: "I can offer a good name, a _certain_ pedigree from the Crusade of Louis the Young, and I know of but thirteen families in Paris that can hold up their heads and say that; but otherwise, I see myself reduced to starvation, to begging my bread; I am a pauper."

This view of life in an elderly man is not calculated to give rise to that meek and philosophic resignation which makes old age cheerful; and but for the outbursts of Commander de Soubirane, a slightly mad and distinctly malicious Southerner, the house in which Octave lived would have been conspicuous, even in the Faubourg Saint-Germain, for its gloom. Madame de Malivert, whom nothing could distract from her anxiety as to her son's health, not even the thought of her own peril, took advantage of the delicate state in which she found herself to cultivate the society of two famous doctors. She sought to win their friendship. As these gentlemen were, one the leader, the other one of the most fervent adherents, of two rival sects, their discussions, albeit of a subject so gloomy to any one who is not animated by an interest in science and in the solution of the problem that faces him, were sometimes amusing to Madame de Malivert, who had not lost a keen and curious mind. She led them on to talk, and thanks to them, now and again at least, voices were raised in the drawing-room, so nobly furnished and yet so sombre, of the Hôtel de Malivert.

Its hangings of green velvet, surcharged with gilded ornaments, seemed to have been put there on purpose to absorb all the light that might come in through two huge windows, the original panes of which had been replaced by plate glass. These windows gave upon a deserted garden, divided into irregular compartments by box hedges. A row of limes, trimmed regularly three times in the year, bounded its farther end, and their motionless shapes seemed a living image of the private lives of the family. The young Vicomte's bedroom, which stood above the drawing-room and had been sacrificed to the beauty of that essential apartment, was barely the height of a half-landing. This room was the bane of Octave's life, and a score of times, in his parents' hearing, he had sung its praises. He lived in dread lest some involuntary exclamation should betray him and reveal how intolerable this room and the whole house were to him.

He keenly regretted his little cell at the Ecole Polytechnique. His time there had been precious to him because it offered him the semblance of the retirement and calm of a monastery. For a long time Octave had had thoughts of withdrawing from the world and of consecrating his life to God. This idea had alarmed his family, especially the Marquis, who saw in the project the fulfilment of all his fears of the abandonment which he dreaded in his old age. But in seeking a closer knowledge of the truths of religion, Octave had been led to study the writers who for the last two centuries have tried to explain the nature of human thought and will, and his ideas had changed considerably; his father's had not changed at all. The Marquis, who had a horror of books and lawyers, was aghast to see this young man shew a passion for reading; he was constantly afraid of some scandal or other, and this was one of his principal reasons for wishing an early marriage for Octave.

While they were basking in the fine days of late autumn, which, in Paris, is like spring, Madame de Malivert said to her son: "You ought to go out riding." Octave saw nothing in this suggestion but an additional expense, and as his father's incessant lamentations made him suppose the family fortune to be far more reduced than it actually was, he held out for a long time. "What is the use, dear Mama," was his invariable reply; "I am quite a tolerable horseman, but riding gives me no pleasure." Madame de Malivert added to the stable a superb English horse, the youth and beauty of which formed a strange contrast to the pair of old Norman horses which for the last twelve years had sufficed for the needs of the household. Octave was embarrassed by this present; the neixt two days he spent in thanking his mother for it; but on the third, happening to be alone with her, when their conversation turned to the English horse: "I love you too well to thank you again," he said, taking Madame de Malivert's hand and pressing it to his lips. "Is your son, for once in his life, to be

wanting in sincerity towards the person he loves most in the world?
This horse is worth 4,000 francs; you are not rich enough to be able
to spend so much money without feeling the want of it."

Madame de Malivert opened the drawer of a writing desk. "Here is my
will," she said; "I have left you my diamonds, but upon the express
condition that as long as the money you receive from the sale of them
shall last, you shall have a horse which you are to ride now and again
by my order. I have sold two of the diamonds secretly to give myself
the pleasure of seeing you on a fine horse in my lifetime. One of the
greatest sacrifices your father has imposed on me has been his making
me promise not to part with these ornaments which become me so ill. He
has some political expectation, which to my mind rests upon a very
slender basis, and he would think himself twice as poor and twice as
decayed on the day when his wife no longer had her diamonds."

A profound melancholy appeared on Octave's brow, and he replaced in
the drawer of the desk that document the name of which reminded him of
so painful, perhaps so imminent an event. He took his mother's hand
again, and held it in both his own, a display of feeling which he
rarely allowed himself. "Your father's plans," Madame de Malivert went
on, "depend upon that Bill of Indemnity of which we have been hearing
for the last three years." "I hope with all my heart that it may be
rejected," said Octave. "And why," his mother Went on, delighted to
see him shew animation at anything and give her this proof of his
esteem and affection, "why should you wish to see it rejected?" "In
the first place, because, not being comprehensive, it seems to me to
be scarcely just; secondly, because it will mean my marrying. I have
the misfortune to have a peculiar nature, I did not create myself so;
all that I have been able to do has been to know myself. Except at
those moments when I have the happiness of being alone with you, my
one pleasure in life consists in living in complete isolation, where
not a living soul has the right to address me." "Dear Octave, this
singular taste is the result of your inordinate passion for learning;
your studies make me tremble; you will end like Goethe's Faust. Are
you prepared to swear to me, as you did on Sunday, that your reading
is not confined to very bad books?" "I read the books that you have
indicated to me, dear Mama, at the same time as those which are called
bad books." "Ah! There is something mysterious and sombre about you
which makes me shudder; heaven only knows what you derive from all
this reading!" "Dear Mama, I cannot refuse to believe in the truth of
what seems to me to be true. How could an all-powerful and good Being

punish me for placing my faith in the evidence of the organs with which He Himself has furnished me?" "Ah! I am always afraid of angering that terrible Being," said Madame de Malivert with tears in her eyes; "He may take you out of reach of my love. There are days when after reading Bourdaloue I am frozen with terror. I find in the Bible that that all-powerful Being is pitiless in His vengeance, and you are doubtless offending Him when you read the philosophers of the eighteenth century. I confess to you, the day before yesterday, I came out of Saint-Thomas d'Aquin in a state bordering on despair. Though the anger of the All-Powerful with impious books were but the tenth part of what M. l'Abbé Fay-------preaches, I might still be afraid of losing you. There is an abominable journal which M. l'Abbé Fay-------durst not even name in his sermon, and which you read every day, I am sure." "Yes, Mama, I do read it, but I am faithful to the promise I gave you; immediately afterwards I read the paper whose doctrine is diametrically opposed to it."

"Dear Octave, it is the violence of your passions that alarms me, and above all the course that they are secretly tracing in your heart. If I saw in you any of the tastes natural at your age, to provide a diversion from your singular ideas, I should be less alarmed. But you read impious books, and presently you will begin to doubt the very existence of God. Why reflect upon these terrible subjects? Do you recall your passion for chemistry? For eighteen months you refused to see anybody, you estranged by your absence our nearest relatives; you failed in the most essential duties." "My interest in chemistry," replied Octave, "was not a passion, it was a duty that I set myself; and heaven knows," he added with a sigh, "whether I should not have done better, by remaining faithful to that plan and making myself a man of learning withdrawn from the world, by following the example of Newton!"

That evening Octave remained with his mother until one o'clock. In vain had she urged him to go out to some social gathering, or at least to the play. "I stay where I feel most happy," said Octave. "There are moments when I believe you, and those are when I am with you," was his delighted mother's answer; "but if for two days on end I have seen you only with other people, my better judgment prevails. It is impossible that such solitude can be good for a boy of your age. I have diamonds here worth 74,000 francs lying idle, and likely to remain so for long, since you shew no intention of marrying; and indeed you are very young, twenty and five days!" here Madame de Malivert rose from her couch to kiss her son. "I have a good mind to sell these useless diamonds, I shall invest what I receive for them, and the interest I shall employ in increasing my expenditure; I should fix a day, and, on the plea of my feeble health, I should be at home to those people only to whom you had no objection." "Alas, dear Mama, the sight of all my fellow créatures depresses me equally; I care for no one in the world but you...."

When her son had left her, notwithstanding the lateness of the hour, Madame de Malivert, troubled by sinister forebodings, was unable to sleep. She tried in vain to forget how dear Octave was to her, and to judge him as she would have judged a stranger. Invariably, instead of following a line of reason, her mind went astray among romantic suppositions as to her son's future; the Commanderas saying recurred to her. "Certainly," she said, "I feel in him something superhuman; he lives like a creature apart, separated from the rest of mankind." Then reverting to more reasonable ideas, Madame de Malivert could not conceive her son's having the liveliest or at least the most exalted passions, and at the same time such an absence of inclination for everything that was real in life. One would have said that his passions had their source elsewhere and rested upon nothing that exists here below. Everything about Octave, even his noble features, alarmed his mother; his fine and tender eyes filled her with terror. They seemed at times to be gazing into heaven and reflecting the bliss that they saw there. A moment later, one read in them the torments of the damned.

One feels a modest reluctance to question a person whose happiness appears so fragile, and his mother often gazed at him without venturing to address him. In his calmer moments, Octave's eyes seemed to be dreaming of an absent happiness; you would have called him a tender heart kept at a great distance from the sole object of its affections. Octave was sincere in his answers to the questions with which his mother plied him, and yet she could not solve the mystery of that profound and often agitated distraction. From his fifteenth year, Octave had been like this, and Madame de Malivert had never thought seriously of any secret passion. Was not Octave master of himself and of his fortune?

She constantly observed that the realities of life, so far from being a source of emotion to her son, had no other effect than to make him lose patience, as though they came to distract him and to tear him in an aggravating fashion from his beloved musings. Apart from the misfortune of this manner of life which seemed to alienate him from his whole environment, Madame de Malivert could not fail to recognise in Octave a strong and upright mind, spirited and honourable. But this mind knew very well the justice of its claim to independence and liberty, and his noble qualities formed a strange alliance with a profundity of dissimulation incredible in a boy of his age. This cruel reality destroyed in an instant all the dreams of happiness which had brought calm to Madame de Malivert's imagination.

Nothing was more irritating to her son, one might say, more odious, for he was incapable of loving or hating by halves, than the society of his uncle the Commander, and yet every one in the household believed that he liked nothing better than to be M. de Soubirane's adversary at chess, or to _saunter_ with him on the boulevard. This was a favourite expression with the Commander, who for all his sixty years had still quite as many pretensions as in 1789; only the fatuity of argument and profundity had taken the place of the affectations of youth, which have at least the excuse of charm and gaiety. This instance of so ready a dissimulation frightened Madame de Malivert. "I have questioned my son as to the pleasure he finds in his uncle's company, and he has told me the truth; but," she said to herself, "who knows whether some strange design may not be lurking in that singular heart? And if I never put any questions to him about the matter, it will never occur to him to speak to me of it. I am a simple woman," Madame de Malivert told herself, "my vision extends only to a few trivial duties within my range. How could I ever dare to think myself capable of giving advice to so strong and singular a creature? I have no friend to consult, endowed with a sufficiently superior judgment; besides, how can I betray Octave's confidence; have I not promised him absolute secrecy?"

When these melancholy reflexions had disturbed her until daybreak, Madame de Malivert concluded, as was her custom, that she ought to employ such influence as she had over her son to make him go frequently to visit Madame la Marquise de Bonnivet. This was her intimate friend and cousin, a woman of the highest position, in whose drawing-room were constantly to be found all the most distinguished elements of society. "My business," Madame de Malivert told herself, "is to pay court to the persons of merit whom I meet at Madame de Bonnivet's, and so find out what they think of Octave." People went to this house to seek the pleasure of being numbered among Madame de Bonnivet's friends, and the support of her husband, a practised courtier burdened with years and honours, and almost as much prized by his master as was that delightful Admiral de Bonnivet, his ancestor, who made François I do so many foolish things and punished himself for them so nobly.

[Footnote: At the battle of Pavia, towards nightfall, seeing that all was lost, the Admiral cried: "Never shall it be said that I survived such a disaster"; and charging with raised visor into the midst of the enemy, had the consolation of killing a number of them before he himself fell pierced by many wounds (February 24, 1525).]

CHAPTER TWO

_Melancholy mark'd him for her own,
whose ambitious heart overrates
the happiness he cannot enjoy_.
   MARLOW.

[Footnote: The first of these lines is taken from the Epitaph in
Gray's _Elegy_, in the notes to which it is not shewn as an
"Imitation." The ascription of the whole passage to Marlow (_sic_) is
probably, therefore, one of Beyle's fantasies.--C. K. S. M.]

The following morning, at eight o'clock, a great upheaval occurred in
the household of Madame de Malivert. All the bells pealed at once.
Presently the old Marquis paid a visit to his wife, who was still in
bed; he himself had wasted no time in dressing. He came and embraced
her with tears in his eyes, "My dear," he said to her, "we shall see
our grandchildren before we die," and the good old man wept copious
tears. "God knows," he added, "that it is not the thought of ceasing
to be a beggar that makes me like this.... The Bill of Indemnity is
certain to pass, and you are to have two millions." At this moment
Octave, for whom the Marquis had sent, knocked at the door; his father
rose and flung himself into his arms. Octave saw tears which he
perhaps misinterpreted, for an almost imperceptible flush appeared on
his pale cheeks. "Draw back the curtains; give me daylight!" said his
mother in a tone of vivacity. "Come here, look at me," she added, in
the same tone, and, without replying to her husband, examined the
imperceptible flush which was dyeing the upper part of Octave's
cheeks. She knew, from her conversations with the doctors, that a
circular patch of red on the cheeks is a symptom of weak lungs; she
trembled for her son's health and gave no more thought to the two
millions of the indemnity.

When Madame de Malivert was reassured, "Yes, my son," the Marquis said
at length, slightly out of patience with all this fuss, "I have just
heard for certain that the Bill of Indemnity is to be introduced, and
we can count upon 319 certain votes out of 420. Your mother has lost a
fortune which I reckon at more than six millions, and whatever may be
the sacrifices which the fear of the Jacobins may impose upon the
King's justice, we may safely count upon two millions. And so I am no
longer a beggar, that is to say, you are no longer a beggar, your
fortune will once again be in keeping with your birth, and I am now in

a position to seek, instead of begging a bride for you." "But, my dear," said Madame de Malivert, "take care that your haste to believe this great news does not expose you to the petty criticisms of our cousin Madame la Duchesse d'Ancre and her friends. She already has all the millions that you promise us; don't count your chickens before they are hatched." "For the last five and twenty minutes," said the old Marquis, taking out his watch, "I have been certain, yes, you may say _certain_, that the Bill of Indemnity will be passed."

The Marquis must have been right, for that evening, when the impassive Octave appeared in Madame de Bonnivet's drawing-room, he found a trace of eagerness in the welcome which he received on all sides.

There was also a trace of pride in his manner of responding to this sudden interest; so at least the old Duchesse d'Ancre remarked. Octave's impression was one of aversion combined with scorn. He found himself greeted more warmly, _because of the prospect of two millions_, in Parisian society, and among the people with whom he had been on most intimate terms. His ardent spirit, as just and almost as severe towards others as towards himself, ended by extracting a profound melancholy from this sad truth. It was not that Octave's pride stooped to resentment of the people whom chance had brought together in this drawing-room; he was filled with pity for his own lot and for that of all mankind. "I am so little loved, then," he said to himself, "that two millions alter all the feelings that people had for me; instead of seeking to deserve their love, I ought to have tried to enrich myself by some form of trade." As he made these gloomy reflexions, Octave happened to be seated upon a divan, facing a little chair which was occupied by Armance de Zohi-loff, his cousin, and by accident his eyes came to rest upon her. It occurred to him that she had not uttered a word to him all that evening. Armance was a niece, in reduced circumstances, of Mesdames de Bonnivet and de Malivert, of about the same age as Octave, and as these two young people were quite indifferent to one another, they were in the habit of conversing with entire frankness. For three-quarters of an hour Octave's heart had been steeped in bitterness, an idea now struck him: "Armance pays me no compliment, she alone of the people here is untouched by this increased interest which I owe to money, she alone here has some nobility of soul." And he found some consolation merely in looking at Armance. "So here at last is a creature worthy of respect," he said to himself, and as the evening advanced, he saw with a pleasure equal to the grief which at first had flooded his heart that she continued to refrain from addressing him.

Once only, when a provincial, a member of the Chamber of Deputies, was paying Octave an ill-turned compliment with regard to the two millions which _he was going to vote him_ (these were the man's own words), Octave caught a glance from Armance directed at himself. Her expression was one that it was impossible to misinterpret; so at least Octave's judgment, more severe than could well be imagined, decided; this glance was intended to study him, and (what gave him a perceptible feeling of pleasure) seemed to expect to be obliged to despise him. The Deputy who was preparing to vote millions received no quarter from Octave; the young Vicomte's scorn was all too visible even to a provincial. "They are all the same," said the Deputy from the--------Department to Commander de Soubirane whom he joined a moment later. "Ah, you fine noblemen of the Court, if we could vote our own indemnities without passing yours, you should not touch a penny, begad, until you had given us guarantees. We have no wish now, as in the old days, to see you colonels at three and twenty and ourselves captains at forty. Of the 319 Deputies who are on the right side, 212 of us belong to that provincial nobility which was sacrificed in the past...." The Commander, highly flattered at hearing such a complaint addressed to himself, began to make excuses for the people of quality. This conversation, which M. de Soubirane in his self-importance called political, lasted for the rest of the evening, and, notwithstanding the most piercing north wind, took place in the bay of a window, the position prescribed for talking politics.

The Commander deserted his post for a minute only, after begging the Deputy to excuse him and to wait for him there. "I must go and ask my nephew what he has done with my carriage," and he went and whispered to Octave: "Talk, people are remarking on your silence; pride is the last thing you should shew at this change of fortune. Remember that these two millions are a restitution and nothing more. Keep your pride till the King gives you a Blue Riband." And the Commander returned to his window, running like a boy, and muttering to himself: "Ah! At half-past eleven, the carriage."

Octave began to talk, and if he did not arrive at the ease and sprightliness which make for complete success, his astonishing good looks and the intense earnestness of his manner made a number of the women present attach an uncommon value to what he said to them. It is true that the noble simplicity with which he uttered his words spoiled the effect of several piquant sallies; it was only after a moment or two that his hearers felt surprise. His proud nature never allowed him to utter in an emphatic tone what he thought effective. His was one of those minds which their natural pride places in the position of a girl who appears without rouge in a drawing-room where the use of rouge is general; for the first few minutes her pallor makes her appear sad. If Octave met with success, it was because the place of the nimble wit and excitement which he often lacked was filled that evening by a sentiment of the bitterest irony.

This semblance of malice led the women of a certain age to pardon him the simplicity of his manners, and the fools whom he frightened made haste to applaud him. Octave, delicately expressing all the contempt that was devouring him, was tasting the only happiness that society could give him, when the Duchesse d'Ancre came up to the divan upon which he was seated and said, not to him but for his benefit, and in the lowest of tones, to her dearest friend Madame de la Ronze: "Look at that little fool Armance, she has actually taken it into her head to be jealous of the fortune that has fallen from the clouds at M. de Malivert's feet. Lord! How ill envy becomes a woman!" Her friend guessed the Duchesse's meaning, and caught the fixed stare of Octave who, while appearing to see nothing but the venerable face of the Bishop of--------who was talking to him at the moment, had heard all. In less than three minutes, Mademoiselle de Zohiloff's silence was explained, and she herself proved guilty, in Octave's mind, of all the base feelings of which she had been accused. "Great God," he said to himself, "there is no exception, then, to the baseness of feeling of all this set! And what grounds have I for supposing that other sets are in any way different? If people dare to flaunt such a worship of money in one of the most exclusive drawing-rooms in France, among people, none of whom can open the History of France without coming upon a hero of his own name, what can it be like among the wretched merchants, who are millionaires to-day, but whose fathers only yesterday were behind the counter? God, how vile men are!"

Octave fled from Madame de Bonnivet's drawing-room; the fashionable world filled him with horror. He left the family carriage for his uncle the Commander and returned home on foot. It was raining in torrents; the rain delighted him. Soon he had ceased to notice the regular tempest that was meanwhile flooding Paris. "The one resource against this general degradation," he thought, "would be to find a noble soul, not yet debased by the sham wisdom of the Duchesse d'Ancre and all her kind, to cling to her forever, to see no one but her, to live with her and solely for her and for her happiness. I should love her passionately. ... _I should love her_! Wretch that I am!" At this moment a carriage turning at a gallop from the Rue de Poitiers into the Rue de Bourbon almost ran over Octave. The back wheel struck him violently in the chest and tore his waistcoat: he stood rooted to the ground; the vision of death had cooled his blood.

"God! Why was I not crushed out of existence?" he said, looking up to heaven. Nor did the rain that was falling in torrents make him bow his head; this cold rain did him good. It was only some minutes later that he proceeded on his way. He ran upstairs to his own room, changed his clothes, and inquired whether his mother were visible. But as she did not expect him she had gone early to bed. Left to his own company, he found everything tedious, even the sombre Alfieri, one of whose tragedies he attempted to read. For a long time he paced the floor of his vast and low apartment. Finally, "Why not make an end of it all?" he asked himself; "why this obstinate resistance to the fate that is crushing me? It is all very well my forming what are apparently the most reasonable plans of conduct, my life is nothing but a succession of griefs and bitter feelings. This month is no better than the last; this year is no better than last year. Why this obstinate determination to go on living? Can I be wanting in firmness? What is death?" he asked himself, opening his case of pistols and examining them. "A very small matter, when all is said; only a fool would be concerned about it. My mother, my poor mother, is dying of consumption; a little time, and I must follow her. I may even precede her if life is too bitter a grief for me. Were it possible to ask such a favour, she would grant it.... The Commander, my father himself do not care for me; they value the name I bear; they cherish in me an excuse for ambition. It is a very minor duty that binds me to them...." This word _duty_ came like a thunderbolt to Octave. "A _minor duty_!" he cried, coming to a halt, "a duty of little importance! ... Is it of little importance, if it is the only duty I have left? If I do not overcome the difficulties that chance presents to me here and now, what right have I to assume that I am certain of conquering all those that it may one day present to me? What! I have the pride to imagine myself superior to every danger, to every sort of evil that may attack a man, and yet I beg the grief that presents itself to choose a form that will suit me, that is to say, to diminish its force by half. What pettiness! And I thought myself so strong! I was nothing but a presumptuous fool."

>From seeing things in this new light to making a vow to overcome the grief of living took only a moment. Soon the disgust which Octave felt at everything became less violent, and he felt himself to be not such a wretched creature. His heart, weighed down and disorganised to some extent by so prolonged an absence of all happiness, regained a little life and courage with the happiness of self-esteem. Ideas of another sort presented themselves. The lowness of the ceiling of his room displeased him intensely; he felt envious of the magnificent saloon of the Hôtel de Bonnivet. "It is at least twenty feet high," he said to himself, "how freely I should breathe in it! Ah!" he exclaimed with the glad surprise of a child, "there is a use for these millions. I shall have a magnificent saloon like the one in the Hôtel de Bonnivet; and only I shall set foot in it. Once a month, at the most, yes, on the first day of the month, a servant to dust it, but in my presence; he must not try to read my thoughts from my selection of books, nor to pry into what I write down for my soul's guidance in its moments of folly.... I shall carry the key always on my watch-chain, a tiny, invisible key of steel, smaller than the key of a portfolio. I shall choose for my saloon three mirrors, each seven feet high. I have always liked that sombre and splendid form of decoration. What is the size of the largest mirrors they make at Saint-Gobain?" And the man who, for the last three-quarters of an hour, had been thinking of ending his life, sprang at once upon a chair to look on his shelves for the price-list of the Saint-Gobain mirrors. He spent an hour in writing out an estimate of the cost of his saloon. He felt that he was behaving like a child; but went on writing all the more rapidly and seriously. This task performed, and the estimate checked, which brought up to 57,350 francs the cost of raising the ceiling of his bedroom and installing a saloon in its place. "If this be not counting one's chickens," he said to himself with a laugh, "I should like to know what is.... Oh, well! I am a miserable wretch!" he went on, striding up and down the room. "Yes, I am a miserable wretch; but I will be stronger than my misery. I shall measure my strength against it, and I shall be the master. Brutus sacrificed his children; that was the difficulty that faced him; as for me, I shall continue to live." He wrote down on a little tablet concealed in the secret drawer of his desk: "December 14th, 182--. _Pleasing effect of two m.--Increase of friendliness.--Envy on the part of Ar.--To make an end.--I will be the master.--Saint-Gobain mirrors_."
This bitter reflexion was written down in Greek characters. Next he

picked out on his piano a whole act of _Don Giovanni_, and those sombre chords of Mozart restored peace to his soul.

CHAPTER THREE

_As the most forward bud Is eaten by the canker ere it blow,
Even so by love the young and tender wit
Is turned to folly....
.... So eating love
Inhabits in the finest wits of all_.
THE TWO GENTLEMEN OF VERONA, Act I.

It was not only at night and when alone that Octave was seized by
these fits of despair. An extreme violence, an extraordinary
spitefulness, marked all his actions at such times, and doubtless, had
he been merely a poor law student without family or friends, he would
have been locked up as a madman. But in that rank of society he would
have had no opportunity of acquiring that elegance of manners which,
adding a final polish to so singular a character, made him a being
apart, even in court circles. Octave was indebted to some extent for
this extreme distinction to the expression of his features; it was
strong and gentle, and not strong and hard, as we see in the majority
of men who are conscious of their good looks. He was naturally
endowed with the difficult art of communicating his thoughts, whatever
they might be, without ever giving offence, or rather without ever
giving unnecessary offence, and thanks to this perfect restraint in
the ordinary relations of life, the idea of his being mad never
suggested itself.

It was less than a year since, seeing that a young footman, alarmed by
the expression on his face, appeared to bar his way, one evening as he
came running out of his mother's drawing-room, Octave in a fury had
cried: "Who are you to stand up to me! If you are strong, shew your
strength." And so saying he had seized him round the body and flung
him out of the window. The footman landed upon a potted oleander in
the garden, without serious injury to himself. For the next two months
Octave appointed himself the man's body servant; in the end he gave
him far too much money, and every day devoted several hours to his
education. The whole family being anxious that this man should keep
silence, presents were given him, and he found himself the object of
excessive attentions which made him a nuisance who had to be sent back
to his home with a pension. The reader can now understand Madame de
Malivert's anxiety.

What had alarmed her most of all at the time of this unfortunate event was that Octave's repentance, albeit extreme, had not begun until the following day. That night, as he returned home, some one having happened to mention to him the danger the man had incurred: "He is young," had been his comment, "why did he not defend himself? When he tried to prevent me from passing, did I not tell him to defend himself?" Madame de Malivert thought she had discovered that these furious outbursts came over her son at the very moments in which he appeared to have most completely forgotten those sombre musings which she could always discern from his expression. It was, for instance, halfway through the performance of a charade, when he had been acting merrily for an hour with several young men and five or six young persons with whom he was intimately acquainted, that he had fled from the drawing-room and hurled the servant out of the window.

Some months before the evening of the two millions, Octave had made almost as abrupt an exit from a ball that Madame de Bonnivet was giving. He had figured with remarkable grace in several country-dances and valses. His mother was delighted with his success, and he himself could not be unaware of it; a number of women for whom their beauty had earned a great celebrity in society, came up and spoke to him with the most flattering air. His hair, of the most beautiful gold, falling in heavy curls over a brow that was really superb, had particularly impressed the celebrated Madame de Claix. And in speaking of the fashions followed by the young men of Naples, where she had just been, she was paying him a marked compliment, when suddenly Octave's face flushed a deep crimson, and he left the room at a pace the swiftness of which he sought in vain to hide. His mother, in alarm, went after him but did not find him. She waited in vain for him all night long; he appeared only the next morning, and in a strange state; he had received three sabre-cuts, which, to tell the truth, were not serious. The doctors were of opinion that this monomania was entirely _moral_ (to use their expression), and must be due not to any physical cause, but to the influence of some singular idea. There was no warning signal of M. le Vicomte Octave's _migraines_, as they were called. These outbursts had been far more common during his first year at the Ecole Polytechnique, and before he had thought of becoming a priest. His fellow-students, with whom he had frequent quarrels, thought him quite mad, and often this conception of him saved him from bodily hurt.

Confined to his bed by the slight injuries of which we have spoken, he had said to his mother, quite simply, as he said everything: "I was furious, I picked a quarrel with some soldiers who were staring at me and laughing, I fought with them, and got no more than I deserve," after which he had changed the subject. With Armance de Zohiloff, his cousin, he had entered into greater detail. "I am subject to moments of misery and fury which are not madness," he said to her one evening, "but which will make me be thought mad in society as I was at the Ecole Polytechnique. It is unfortunate, that is all; but what I cannot face is the fear of finding myself suddenly burdened with some cause for everlasting regret, as nearly happened at the time of poor Pierre's accident." "You made a noble reparation for that, you gave him not only a pension but your time, and if he had had the least spark of decent feeling in him you would have made his fortune. What more could you do?" "Nothing, I dare say, once the accident had happened, or I should be a monster not to have done it. But that is not all, these fits of despondency which every one takes for madness, seem to make me a creature apart. I see the poorest, the most limited, the most wretched, outwardly, of the young men of my generation each blessed with one or two lifelong friends who share his joys and sorrows. In the evening I see them go out and take the air together, and they tell one another everything that interests them; I and I only find myself isolated, without a friend in the world. I have not, nor shall I ever have any one to whom I can freely confide what is in my mind. What outlet should I have for my feelings if I had any of the sort that wring the heart! Am I then fated to live always without friends, and with barely an acquaintance! Am I an evil-doer?" he added, with a sigh. "Certainly not, but you furnish the people who do not like you with pretexts," Armance said to him in the free, severe tone of friendship, and trying to hide the all too real pity which his grief inspired in her. "For instance, you who are so perfectly polite towards everybody, why did you not shew yourself the day before yesterday at Madame de Claix's ball?"

"Because it was her foolish compliments at the ball six months ago that put me to the shame of being worsted by two young peasants armed with sabres."

"That is all very well," Mademoiselle de Zohiloff retorted; "but pray observe that you always find reasons to excuse yourself from going into society. You must not go on to complain of the isolation in which you live." "Ah, it is friends that I need, and not society. Is it among the drawing-rooms that I shall find a friend?" "Yes, since you did not succeed in finding one at the École Polytechnique." "You are right," Octave replied after a long silence; "I see your point of view for the moment, and to-morrow, when it is a question of acting, I shall act in a manner the opposite of that which seems reasonable to me to-day, and entirely from pride! Ah, if heaven had made me the son of a linen-draper, I should have worked in the counting-house from the age of sixteen; instead of which all my occupations have been mere luxury; I should-be less proud and more happy.... Ah! how I detest myself!..."

These complaints, albeit apparently selfish, interested Armance; Octave's eyes expressed such possibilities of love, and were at times so tender!

She, without clearly explaining it to herself, felt that Octave was the victim of that sort of unreasoning sensibility which makes men wretched and worthy to be loved. A passionate imagination led him to exaggerate the happiness which he could not enjoy. Had he received from heaven a dry, cold, reasoning heart, had he been born at Geneva; then, with all the other advantages which he did possess, he might have been quite happy. All that he lacked was an ordinary nature.

It was only in the company of his cousin that Octave ventured now and again to express his thoughts aloud. We see now why he had been so painfully affected on discovering that this charming cousin's sentiments had changed with his change of fortune.

On the morning after the day on which Octave had longed for death, he was awakened with a start at seven o'clock by his uncle the Commander, who entered his room making as much noise as possible. The man was never free from affectation. Octave's anger at this noise lasted for barely a few seconds; a sense of duty recurred to him, and he greeted M. de Soubirane in the light and pleasant tone which seemed best suited to his mood.

This vulgar soul who, before or after good birth, could think of nothing in the world but money, explained at length to the noble Octave that he must not go altogether out of his mind with joy when he passed from an income of twenty-five thousand livres to the prospect of one hundred thousand. This philosophical and almost Christian discourse ended with the advice to speculate on 'Change as soon as he should have secured a twentieth part of his two millions. The Marquis would not fail to place part of this increased fortune at Octave's disposal; but he was on no account to operate on 'Change save by the Commander's advice; the latter knew Madame la Comtesse de-------, and they could speculate in the Funds _with certainty_. These last words made Octave start. "Yes, my boy," said the Commander, who mistook this movement for a sign of doubt, "_with certainty_. I have rather neglected the Comtesse since her absurd behaviour with M. le Prince de S------; still, we are more or less related, and I shall leave you now to go and find our friend in common, the Duc de-------, who will bring us together again."

CHAPTER FOUR

Half a dupe, half duping, The first deceived
perhaps by her deceit And fair words, as all
these philosophers. Philosophers they say?
Mark this, Diego, The devil can cite scripture
for his purpose. Oh, what a goodly outside
falsehood hath!
  MASSINGER.

[Footnote: This motto is printed in the French editions as prose. The
last two lines are taken from _The Merchant of Venice_, Act I, Scene
III, where Antonio says: "Mark you this, Bassanio, The devil," etc.
The ascription to Massinger need not be taken too seriously. Compare
Scarlet and Black, Chapter XLVI.--C. K. S. M.]

This fatuous invasion by the Commander almost plunged Octave back in
his misanthropy of overnight. His disgust with the rest of mankind had
risen to a climax when his servant appeared carrying a stout volume
very carefully wrapped in English tissue paper. The seal it bore had
been beautifully engraved, but the blazon itself was somewhat
repellent: sable, two bones in saltire. Octave, whose taste was
perfect, admired the accuracy of outline of this pair of tibias and
the perfection of the engraver's skill. "It is the School of Pikler,"
he said to himself; "this must be one of my cousin, the devout Madame
de C------'s follies." This suspicion proved unfounded when he saw
inside the parcel a magnificent copy of the Bible, bound by Thouvenin.
"Devout Catholics do not give one the Bible," said Octave as he opened
the accompanying letter; but he sought in vain for the signature;
there was none, and he tossed the letter unread into the grate. A
moment later, his servant, old Saint-Jacques, entered the room with an
air of cunning. "Who sent me this parcel?" said Octave. "It is a
mystery, they are trying to keep it secret from M. le Vicomte; but it
was simply old Perrin who left it with the porter and made off like a
pickpocket." "And who is old Perrin?" "One of Madame la Marquise de
Bonnivet's servants whom she pretended to dismiss and now uses for
secret errands." "Do you mean that people suspect Madame de Bonnivet
of a love-affair?" "Good heavens, no, Sir. The secret errands are for
the new religion. It is a Bible, perhaps, that Madame la Marquise has
sent to Monsieur as a great secret. Monsieur perhaps recognized the
writing of Madame Rouvier, Madame la Marquise's confidential maid."

Octave looked in the grate and made the man give him back the letter which had fallen behind the fire and was not burned. He saw with surprise that the writer knew quite well that he read Helvetius, Bentham, Bayle and other bad books. "The most spotless virtue would not be safe," he said to himself; "as soon as people form a sect, they stoop to the use of intrigue and employ spies. It is evidently since the Bill of Indemnity was introduced that I have become worthy that people should take an interest in my salvation and the influence that I may one day wield."

Throughout that day, the conversation of the Marquis de Malivert, the Commander and two or three trusted friends who were invited to dine Was an almost incessant allusion, in distinctly bad taste, to Octave's marriage and to his new position. Being still affected by the spiritual crisis through which he had passed during the night, he was less frigid than usual. His mother thought him paler, and he made it his duty, if not to be gay, at least to appear to be occupying himself only with ideas that gave rise to pleasing pictures; he set himself to the task with so much energy that he succeeded in taking in every one in the room. Nothing could deter him, not even the Commander's pleasantries touching the prodigious effect produced by two millions on the mind of a philosopher. Octave took advantage of his feigned bewilderment to say that, were he a Prince, he would not marry before he was twenty-six, this being the age at which his father had married.

"It is evident that the fellow is nourishing the secret ambition of becoming a Bishop or a Cardinal," said the Commander as soon as Octave had left the room; "his birth and sound doctrine will carry him to the Hat." This speech, which made Madame de Malivert smile, caused the Marquis great uneasiness. "You may say what you please," he replied to his wife's smile, "my son's only intimate relations are with churchmen or young scholars of the same way of thinking, and, a thing that is quite unknown in my family, he shews a marked dislike for officers of his own age." "There is something strange about that young man," M. de Soubirane went on. At this reflexion it was Madame de Malivert's turn to sigh.

Octave, overcome by the boredom with which the obligation to talk had filled him, left this group of old people and went at an early hour to the Gymnase: he could not endure the wit of M. Scribe's amusing plays. "Still," he told himself, "nothing else has had so genuine a success, and to despise a thing without knowing it is an absurdity too common in our society for me to acquire any credit by avoiding it." It was in vain that he prolonged the experiment through two of the most charming sketches given at the Theatre de Madame. The wittiest and most amusing lines seemed to him to be tainted with vulgarity, and the handing over of the key in the second act of _Le Mariage de Raison_ drove him from the theatre. He entered a restaurant and, faithful to the mystery which enveloped all his actions, called for candles and a plate of soup: when the soup was put before him, he locked the door, read with interest two newspapers which he had bought outside, burned them with the greatest care in the grate, paid his bill and left. He went home and changed his clothes, and found himself almost eager that evening to put in an appearance at Madame de Bonnivet's. "How can I be certain," he wondered, "that that wicked Duchesse d'Ancre was not slandering Mademoiselle de Zohiloff? My uncle is convinced that my head has been turned by those two millions." This idea, which had been suggested to Octave by something of no importance that he had read in one of his newspapers, restored his happiness. He thought still of Armance, but as of his only friend, or rather the only person who was almost a friend to him.

He was far from imagining himself to be in love, he had a horror of that sentiment. He had sworn to himself a thousand times in the last four years that he would never love. This obligation to refrain from love was the mainspring of his whole conduct and the chief occupation of his life. This evening, his soul strengthened by virtue and misery, and become merely virtue and strength, felt simply the fear of having too lightly condemned _a friend_.

On reaching Madame de Bonnivet's drawing-room, Octave did not once look at Armance; but throughout the evening his eyes did not miss a single one of her movements. He began, upon entering the room, by paying marked attention to the Duchesse d'Ancre; he spoke to her with a deference so profound that the lady had the pleasure of supposing him to be converted to the respect due to her rank. "Now that he has the prospect of becoming rich, this philosopher is one of us," she murmured to Madame de la Ronze.

Octave wished to make certain of the extent of this woman's perversity; if he found that she was really wicked, that would be to some extent an admission that Mademoiselle de Zohiloff was innocent. He observed that the feeling of hatred alone retained some animation in the withered heart of Madame d'Ancre; whereas, on the other hand, only things that were generous and noble inspired her with revulsion. One would have said that she felt the need to be avenged on them.

Ignoble and base sentiments, but ignobility clothed in the most elegant expressions, had alone the privilege of making the Duchesse's little eyes sparkle.

Octave was thinking of how to free himself from the interest with which she was listening to him when he heard Madame de Bonnivet call for her chessmen. These were a little masterpiece of carved ivory which M. l'Abbé Dubois had brought from Canton. Octave seized the opportunity to leave Madame d'Ancre, and asked his cousin to entrust him with the key of the desk in which her fear of her servants' clumsiness made her keep these magnificent chessmen. Armance was no longer in the room; she had gone out a few moments earlier with Méry de Tersan, her bosom friend; had not Octave asked for the key of the desk, the absence of Mademoiselle de Zohiloff would have given rise to unfavourable comment, and on her return she might perhaps have had to endure several hostile glances, perfectly restrained, but distinctly harsh. Armance was penniless; she was only eighteen, and Madame de Bonnivet was thirty and more; she was still quite a beautiful woman, but Armance, too, was beautiful.

The two friends had stopped by the chimneypiece of a large boudoir that opened out of the drawing-room. Armance had wished to shew Méry a portrait of Lord Byron a proof of which Mr. Phillips, the English painter, had recently sent to her aunt. Octave could hear quite distinctly as he passed along the passage by the door of the boudoir: "What can you expect? He is like all the rest! A soul that I thought so noble overpowered by the prospect of two millions!" The accent in which these flattering words, _that I thought so noble_, were uttered, fell on Octave like a bolt from the blue; he stood rooted to the ground. When he moved on, his tread was so light that the sharpest ear could not have caught it. As he passed again by the boudoir with the chessmen in his hand, he stopped for a moment; immediately he blushed at his indiscretion and returned to the drawing-room. The words which he had just overheard were by no means decisive in a world in which envy is capable of assuming every imaginable form; but the accent of candour and honesty in which they had been uttered echoed in his heart. That was not the tone of envy.

Having handed the Chinese chessmen to his cousin, Octave felt that he needed time for reflexion; he took up a position in a corner of the room behind a whist-table, and there his imagination repeated to him a score of times the sound of the words he had just overheard. This profound and delicious meditation had long absorbed him, when the voice of Armance came to his ear. He had not yet thought what means to employ to regain his cousin's esteem; he was still lost in ecstatic enjoyment of the bliss of having forfeited it. As he rejoined the group that surrounded Madame de Bonni-vet, and came away from the remote corner occupied by the tranquil whist-players, Armance noticed the expression in his eyes; they rested upon her with that sort of tenderness and weariness which, after intense joys, makes the eyes seem almost incapable of unduly rapid movements.

Octave was not to find happiness a second time that evening; he could not address a single word to Armance. "Nothing could be harder than to justify myself," he said to himself while pretending to be listening to the exhortations of the Duchesse d'Ancre who, being with him the last to leave the drawing-room, insisted upon taking him home. The night was cold and dry with a brilliant moon; on reaching home, Octave called for his horse and rode for some miles along the new boulevard. On his return, about three o'clock in the morning, without knowing what he was doing or why, he passed before the Hôtel de Bonnivet,

CHAPTER FIVE

_Her glossy hoar was cluster'd o'er a brow
Bright with intelligence, and fair, and smooth;
Her eyebrows' shape was like th' aerial bow,
Her cheek all purple with the beam of youth,
Mounting, at times, to a transparent glow,
As if her veins ran lightning_ ....
   DON JUAN, I, 61.

"How am I to prove to Mademoiselle de Zohiloff, by deeds and not by
vain words, that the pleasure of seeing my father's fortune multiplied
fourfold has not absolutely turned my head?" The search for an answer
to this question was Octave's sole occupation during the next
twenty-four hours. For the first time in his life, he had lost his
heart without knowing it.

For many years past, he had always been conscious of his own
sentiments, and had confined their attention to the objects that
seemed to him reasonable. Now, on the other hand, it was with all the
impatience of a boy of twenty that he waited for the hour at which he
was to meet Mademoiselle de Zohiloff. He had no longer the slightest
doubt as to the possibility of speaking to a person whom he saw twice
almost every day; he was embarrassed only over the selection of the
words best fitted to convince her. "For, really," he said, "I cannot
within twenty-four hours perform an action that will prove in a
decisive manner that I am above the pettiness of which in her heart of
hearts she accuses me, and I must be allowed to protest first of all
in words." And indeed an abundance of words presented themselves to
him in turn; some seemed to him to be over-emphatic; at other moments
he was afraid of treating too lightly so serious an imputation. He had
not in the least decided what he ought to say to Mademoiselle de
Zohiloff when eleven struck, and he arrived among the first visitors
in the drawing-room of the Hôtel de Bonnivet. But what was his
astonishment when he discovered that Mademoiselle de Zohiloff, who
spoke to him several times in the course of the evening, and
apparently quite in her ordinary tone, deprived him nevertheless of
any opportunity of saying a word to her which no one else might hear!
Octave was greatly vexed, the evening passed in a flash.

On the following day he was equally unfortunate; next day again, and
for many days after that, he was prevented from speaking to Armance.

Each day he hoped to find an opportunity of saying the words that were so essential to his honour, and each day, without there being the slightest sign of affectation in Mademoiselle de Zohiloff's behaviour, he saw his hope vanish. He was losing the friendship and esteem of the one person who seemed to him worthy of his own, because he was suspected of sentiments the opposite to those that he actually held. Nothing really could have been more flattering, but at the same time nothing was more annoying. Octave was intensely preoccupied in what was happening to him; it took him several days to grow accustomed to his new position of disfavour with Armance. Quite unconsciously, he who had so loved silence acquired the habit of talking volubly whenever Mademoiselle de Zohiloff was within earshot. In truth, it mattered little to him though he seemed odd or inconsequent. Whatever brilliant or eminent lady he might be addressing, he spoke really to Mademoiselle de Zohiloff alone, and for her benefit.

This real misfortune distracted Octave from his black misery, he forgot his habit of seeking always to estimate the amount of happiness that he was enjoying at the moment. He was losing his one friend; he saw himself refused an esteem which he was so certain that he deserved; but these misfortunes, cruel as they might be, did not go so far as to inspire in him that profound distaste for life which he had felt a fortnight earlier. He asked himself: "What man is there who has not been slandered? The severity with which I am treated is an earnest of the eagerness with which the injury will be repaired when the truth shall at last be known."

Octave could see an obstacle that kept him from happiness, but he could also see happiness, or at least the end of his suffering and of a suffering that completely absorbed his thoughts. His life had a new object, he longed passionately to reconquer the esteem of Armance; it was no easy undertaking. The girl had a strange nature. Born on the outskirts of the Russian Empire near the Caucasian frontier, at Se-bastopol where her father was in command, Mademoiselle de Zohiloff concealed beneath an apparent meekness a firm will, worthy of the rugged clime in which she had spent her childhood. Her mother, who was closely related to Mesdames de Bonnivet and de Malivert, had when attached to the Court of Louis XVIII at Mitau, married a Russian colonel. M. de Zohiloff came of a family which for the last hundred years had obtained the highest preferments; but the father and grandfather of this officer, having had the misfortune to attach themselves to favourites who were shortly afterwards banished to

Siberia, had seen their fortune rapidly diminish.

Armance's mother died in 1811; shortly afterwards she lost General de Zohiloff, her father, who was killed at the battle of Montmirail. Madame de Bonnivet, on learning that she had a relative living alone and friendless in a small town in the heart of Russia, with no fortune beyond an income of one hundred louis, did not hesitate to invite her to France. She spoke of her as a niece and reckoned upon marrying her by obtaining some pension from the Court; Armance's maternal great-grandfather had worn the Blue Riband. We see that, though barely eighteen, Mademoiselle de Zohiloff had already had sufficient experience of misfortune. This perhaps was why the minor events of life seemed to glide over her, leaving her unmoved. Now and again it was not impossible to read in her eyes that she was capable of being deeply affected, but one could see that nothing vulgar would succeed in touching her. This perfect serenity, which it would have been so gratifying to make her forget for a moment, was combined in her with the subtlest intellect, and entitled her to a consideration beyond her years.

She was indebted to this singular nature, and above all to the enchanting gaze of a pair of large, deep blue eyes, for the friendship of all the most eminent ladies in Madame de Bonnivet's circle; but Mademoiselle de Zohiloff had also a number of enemies. In vain had her aunt tried to force her out of her sheer incapacity to bestow her attention upon people whom she did not like. It was all too evident that in speaking to them she was thinking of something else. There were, moreover, any number of little tricks of speech and behaviour which Armance would not have ventured to condemn in other women; possibly it never occurred to her to forbid herself the use of them; but had she allowed herself that liberty, for long afterwards she would have blushed whenever she thought of them. In her childhood, her feelings with regard to childish trifles had been so violent that she had strongly reproached herself for them. She had formed the habit of criticising herself with reference not to the effect she produced on others but to her sentiments at the moment, the memory of which next day might be the bane of her life.

People found something Asiatic in the features of this girl, as in her gentleness and a carelessness which seemed to belie her age, so childish was it. None of her actions gave any direct indication of an exaggerated sense of what a woman owes to herself, and yet a certain graceful charm, an enchanting reserve, was diffused round about her.

Without seeking in any way to attract attention, and letting opportunities of success escape her at every moment, the girl was interesting. One could see that Armance did not allow herself a whole crowd of things which custom has authorised and which are to be observed every day in the conduct of the most distinguished women. In short, I have no doubt that, but for her extreme gentleness and her youth, Mademoiselle de Zohiloff's enemies would have accused her of being a prude.

Her education abroad, and her belated arrival in France, served as a further excuse for whatever slight oddity the eye of malice might have discovered in her manner of being impressed by events, and indeed in her behaviour generally.

Octave spent his life among the enemies which this unusual nature had created for Mademoiselle de Zohiloff; the marked favour which she enjoyed with Madame de Bonnivet was a grievance which the friends of that lady, so important a figure in society, could not forgive her. It was above all things her unswerving honesty that alarmed them. As it is far from easy to attack the actions of a young girl, they attacked her beauty. Octave was the first to admit that his young cousin might easily have been far better looking. She was remarkable for what I might perhaps venture to call Russian beauty: this was a combination of features which, while expressing to a marked degree a simplicity and piety no longer to be found among over-civilised races, offered, one must confess, a singular blend of the purest Circassian beauty with certain German forms somewhat prematurely developed. There was nothing common in the outline of those features, so profoundly serious, but a little too full of expression, even in repose, to correspond exactly to the idea generally held in France of the beauty becoming to a young girl.

It is a great advantage, with generous natures, to the people who are accused in their hearing, that those people's faults should be pointed out first of all by the lips of an enemy. When the hatred of Madame de Bonnivet's bosom friends deigned to stoop to open jealousy of the poor little existence of Armance, they never ceased to mock at the bad effect produced by the too prominent brow and by features which, seen in full face, were perhaps a little too strongly marked.

The only real grounds for attack which the expression of Armance's countenance could offer to her enemies was a singular look which she had at times when her mind was most detached. This fixed and profound gaze was one of extreme attention; there was nothing in it, certainly, that could shock the most severe delicacy; it suggested neither coquetry nor assurance; but no one could deny that it was singular, and, in that respect, out of place in a young person. Madame de Bonnivet's flatterers, when they were sure of being noticed, would sometimes imitate this look, in discussing Armance among themselves; but these vulgar spirits robbed it of an element that they had never thought of noticing. "It is with such eyes," Madame de Mali-vert said to them one day, out of patience with their malevolence, "that a pair of angels exiled among men and obliged to disguise themselves in mortal form, would gaze at one another in mutual recognition."

It will be admitted that with a character so steadfast in its beliefs and so frank as was that of Armance, it was no easy matter to justify oneself against a grave charge by adroit hints. Octave would have required, to be successful, a presence of mind and above all a degree of assurance which were beyond his years.

Unconsciously Armance allowed him to see, by a casual utterance, that she no longer looked upon him as an intimate friend; his heart was wrung, he remained speechless for a quarter of an hour. He was far from discovering in the form of Armance's speech a pretext for replying to it in an effective manner and so recovering his rights. Now and again he attempted to speak, but it was too late, and his reply was no longer appropriate; still, it did shew that he was concerned. While seeking in vain for a way of justifying himself in face of the accusation which Armance brought against him in secret, Octave let it be seen, quite unconsciously, how deeply it affected him; this was perhaps the most skilful method of winning her forgiveness.

Now that the course to be adopted with regard to the Bill of Indemnity was no longer a secret, even from society as a whole, Octave, greatly to his surprise, found that he had become a sort of personage. He saw himself made an object of attention by serious people. He was treated in quite a novel fashion, especially by very great ladies who might see in him a possible match for their daughters. This mania of the mothers of the period, to be constantly in pursuit of a son-in-law, shocked Octave to a degree which it is difficult to express. The Duchesse de-------, to whom he had the honour to be distantly related, thought it necessary to apologise to him for not having kept him a place in a box which she had engaged at the Gymnase for the following evening. "I know, my dear cousin," she said to him, "how unfair you are to that charming theatre, the only one that I find amusing." "I

admit my error," said Octave, "the dramatists are right, and their
witty speeches are not tainted with vulgarity; but the object of this
retractation is by no means to beg you for a place. I admit that I am
not made for society, nor for that kind of play which, evidently, is
the most lifelike copy of it." This misanthropic tone, in so handsome
a young man, appeared highly ridiculous to the Duchesse's two
grand-daughters, who made fun of him for the rest of the evening, but
nevertheless on the following day treated Octave with _perfect
sim-plicity_. He observed this change and shrugged his shoulders.
Astounded by his successes, and even more by their requiring so little
effort on his part, Octave, who was very strong on the theory of life,
expected to have to meet the attacks of envy; "for unquestionably," he
told himself, "this Indemnity must procure me that pleasure also." He
had not long to wait; a few days later, he was informed that some
young officers of Madame de Bonnivet's circle were only too ready to
mock at his change of fortune. "What a misfortune for that poor
Malivert," said one, "these two millions falling on his head like a
chimney-can! He won't be able to become a priest now! It is hard!"
"One fails to conceive," put in a second, "that in this age when the
nobility is so savagely attacked, a man can dare to bear a title and
yet shrink from his baptism of blood." "Still, that is the only virtue
which the Jacobin party has not yet thought of calling hypocritical,"
added a third.
Fired by these remarks, Octave began to go about more, appeared in all
the ballrooms, was very haughty and even, so far as it lay in his
power, impertinent to other young men; but this produced no effect.
Greatly to his astonishment (he was only twenty), he found that people
respected him all the more for this attitude. As a matter of fact, it
was generally decided that the Indemnity had absolutely turned his
head; but most of the women went on to say: "The only thing he lacked
was that proud, independent air!" It was the name which they were
pleased to give to what seemed to him insolence, which he would never
have allowed himself to display had he not been told of the
ill-natured remarks that were being made about him. Octave enjoyed
the surprising welcome which he received in society and which went so
well with that tendency to hold himself aloof which was natural to
him. His success pleased him most of all on account of the happiness
which he discerned in his mother's eyes; it was in answer to repeated
pressure from Madame de Malivert that he had abandoned his beloved
solitude. But the most usual effect of the attentions of which he saw

himself made the object was to remind him of his disfavour with Mademoiselle de Zohiloff. This seemed to increase day by day. There were moments when this disfavour almost bordered upon incivility, it was at all events the most decided aloofness, and was all the more marked inasmuch as the new existence which Octave owed to the Indemnity was nowhere more evident than at the Hôtel de Bonnivet. Now that he might one day find himself the host in an influential drawing-room, the Marquise was absolutely determined to wean him from that arid philosophy of _utility_. This was the name which she had given for some months past to what is ordinarily called the philosophy of the eighteenth century. "When will you throw on the fire," she said to him, "the books of those gloomy writers which you alone, of all the young men of your age and rank, still read?"

It was to a sort of German mysticism that Madame de Bonnivet hoped to convert Octave. She deigned to examine him, to see whether he possessed the _sense of religion_. Octave reckoned this attempt at conversion among the strangest of the things that had happened to him, since his emerging from the solitary life. "Here is one of the follies," he thought, "which no one could ever foresee."

Madame la Marquise de Bonnivet might be reckoned one of the most remarkable women in societj'. Features of a perfect regularity, very large eyes, with the most imposing gaze, a superb figure and manners that were distinctly noble, a little too noble, perhaps, placed her in the highest rank wherever she might be found. Rooms of a certain vastness were especially favourable to Madame de Bonnivet; for instance, on the day of the opening of the final session of the Chambers, she had been the first to be mentioned among the most brilliant women present. Octave saw with pleasure the effect that would be created by her researches into his _sense of religion_. This creature, who imagined himself to be so free from shams, could not restrain a start of pleasure at the sight of a sham which the world would shortly be placing to his credit.

Madame de Bonnivet's exalted virtue was beyond the reach of slander. Her imagination was occupied exclusively with God and the Angels, or at the lowest with certain intermediary beings between God and man, who, according to the most modern German philosophers, hover a few feet above our heads. It is from this elevated though not remote station that they _magnetise our souls_, etc., etc. These visions, in a woman so highly esteemed, were most distressing to His Grace the Archbishop. "The reputation for wisdom which Madame de Bonnivet has enjoyed, upon such good grounds, since her entry into society, and which all the cunning innuendo of the Jesuits in lay clothing has been powerless to assail, she is going to risk for my sake," Octave told himself, and the pleasure of attracting in a marked fashion the attention of so important a woman made him endure with patience the long explanations which she deemed necessary to his conversion. Presently, among his new acquaintance, Octave was marked down as the inseparable companion of that Marquise de Bonnivet, so famous in a certain section of society, and (or so she thought) creating a sensation at Court when she deigned to appear there. Although the Marquise was a very great lady in the height of the fashion, and moreover was still very good looking, these advantages made no impression upon Octave; unfortunately he detected a trace of affectation in her manner, and whenever he observed this defect anywhere, his natural instinct was only to deride it. But this sage of twenty summers was far from penetrating the true cause of the pleasure which he found in letting himself be converted. He, who so many times had taken vows against love, that one might say that hatred of that passion was the main object of his life, went with pleasure to the Hôtel de Bonnivet because invariably that Armance who despised him, who hated him perhaps, was stationed within a few feet of her aunt. Octave was quite free from presumption; the principal flaw in his character indeed that he exaggerated his own disadvan-e7 tages, but if he did admire himself at all, it was in respect of his honesty and stoutness of heart. He had rid himself, without the least ostentation or weakness, of--a number of opinions, ridiculous but agreeable enough in themselves, which are guiding principles to the majority of young men of his class and age.

These victories which he could not conceal from himself, that for instance over his love of a military career, independent of any ambition for military rank and promotion, these victories, I repeat, had inspired him with great confidence in his own firmness. "It is from cowardice and not from want of enlightenment that we do not read in our own hearts," he was in the habit of saying, and with the help of this fine principle, he relied a little too much on his own perspicacity. A chance word informing him that one day he might be in love with Mademoiselle de Zohiloff would have made him leave Paris immediately: but in his present position such an idea never occurred to him. He esteemed Armance highly and so to speak exclusively; he saw himself scorned by her, and he esteemed her precisely on account of her scorn. Was it not quite natural to wish to regain her esteem? There was, underlying this, no suspicious desire to attract the girl. What was calculated to prevent the very birth of the slightest suspicion of love for her was that when Octave found himself among Mademoiselle de Zohiloff's enemies he was the first to admit her defects. But the state of uneasiness and hope, doomed to incessant disappointment, in which his cousin's silent treatment of him kept him plunged prevented him from seeing that none of the faults with which she was reproached in his hearing amounted to anything serious in his mind.

One day, for instance, they were attacking Armance's predilection for hair cut short and falling in thick curls round the head, as worn in Moscow. "Mademoiselle de Zohiloff finds the fashion convenient," said one of the Marquise's flatterers; "she does not wish to sacrifice too much time to her toilet." Octave's malicious spirit noticed with pleasure the success which this argument achieved among society women. They let it be understood that Armance did right to sacrifice everything to the duties which her devotion to her aunt imposed upon her; and their eyes seemed to be saying: "to sacrifice everything to her duties as paid companion." Octave's pride was far from thinking of replying to this insinuation. While they in their malice enjoyed it, he yielded in silence and delight to a little start of passionate admiration. He felt, without expressing it to himself: "This woman who is attacked thus by all the rest is nevertheless the only one here who is worthy of my esteem! She is as poor as these other women are rich; and she alone might be permitted to exaggerate the importance of money. And yet she despises it, she who has not a thousand crowns a year; and it is solely and basely adored by these women, all of whom are living in the greatest comfort."

CHAPTER SIX

Cromwell, I charge thee, fling away ambition;
By that sin fell the angels, how can man then,
The image of his Maker, hope to win by't?
  KING HENRY VIII, Act III.

One evening, after the tables had been arranged and the great ladies
arrived for whom Madame de Bonnivet put herself out, she talked to
Octave with an unusual interest: "I do not understand your nature,"
she repeated for the hundredth time. "If you will swear to me," he
replied, "never to betray my secret, I will confide in you; and no one
else has ever known it." "What! Not even Madame de Malivert?" "My
respect for her forbids me to distress her." Madame de Bonnivet, in
spite of all the idealism of her faith, was by no means insensible of
the charm of knowing the great secret of one of the men who, in her
eyes, came nearest to perfection; besides, this secret had never been
confided to any one.

Upon Octave's requesting an eternal discretion, Madame de Bonnivet
left the drawing-room and after a while returned, wearing upon the
gold chain of her watch a singular ornament: this was a sort of cross
of iron made at Kônigsberg; she held it in her left hand and said to
Octave in a low and solemn tone: "You ask me for eternal secrecy; in
all circumstances, towards every one in the world. With no mental
reservation or Jesuitical pretermission, _I declare to you by
Jehovah_, yes, I will keep your secret."

"Very well, Madame," said Octave, amused by this little ceremony and
by the sacramental air of his noble cousin, "what often clouds my soul
with darkness, what I have never confided to any one, is this horrible
misfortune: I have no _conscience_. I find in myself no trace of what
you call the _intimate sense_, no _instinctive_ revulsion from crime.
If I abhor vice, it is quite vulgarly by force of reason and because I
find it harmful. And what proves to me that there is absolutely
nothing divine or _instinctive_ in my nature, is that I can always
recall all the elements of the reasoning by dint of which I find vice
to be horrible." "Ah, how I pity you, my dear cousin! You distress
me," said Madame de Bonnivet in a tone that revealed the keenest
pleasure; "yours is precisely what we call the _rebellious nature_."

At this moment, her interest in Octave was plain to the eyes of
several malicious watchers; for they were being watched. Her gestures

shed all their affectation and became passionate and genuine; her eyes
darted a mild flame as she listened to this handsome young man; still
more, when she commiserated him. Madame de Bonnivet's good friends,
who were watching her from a distance, indulged in the most rash
judgments, whereas she was merely transported by the pleasure of
having at last found a _rebellious nature_. Octave promised her a
memorable victory if she succeeded in awakening in him conscience and
the _intimate sense_. A celebrated Doctor of the last century,
summoned to the bedside of a great nobleman, his friend, after
examining the symptoms of the disease, slowly and in silence,
exclaimed in a sudden transport of joy: "Ah! Monsieur le Marquis, it
is a disease that has been lost for centuries! Vitreous phlegm! A
superb disease, absolutely fatal. Ah! I have discovered it, I have
discovered it!" Such was the joy of Madame de Bonnivet; it was in a
sense the joy of an artist.
Since she had been engaged in spreading the new Protestantism, which
is to take the place of Christianity, the latter being now a thing of
the past, and, as we know, on the point of undergoing its fourth
metamorphosis, she had heard mention of _rebellious natures_; they
form the solitary objection to the system of German mysticism, founded
upon the existence of the intimate consciousness of good and evil. She
now had the good fortune to have discovered one; she alone in the
world knew his secret. And this _rebellious_ nature was perfect; for
his moral conduct being strictly honourable, no suspicion of personal
interest could taint the purity of his _diabolism_.
I shall not repeat any of the sound reasons which Madame de Bonnivet
advanced that evening to Octave to persuade him that he had an
intimate sense. The reader has not, perhaps, the good fortune to be
seated within a few feet of a charming cousin who despises him with
all her heart and whose friendship he is burning to reconquer. This
intimate sense, as its name implies, cannot manifest itself by any
outward sign; but nothing could be simpler or easier to understand,
said Madame de Bonnivet; "you are a _rebellious nature_," etc., etc.
"Do you not see, do you not feel, that, apart from space and time,
there is nothing real here below?"
Throughout the course of these sound arguments, a joy that was really
almost diabolical sparkled in the glance of the Vicomte de Malivert;
and Madame de Bonnivet, who for that matter was a most perspicacious
woman, exclaimed: "Ah, my dear Octave, _rebellion_ is evident in your
eyes." It must be admitted that those great dark eyes, which as a rule

shewed such discouragement, and whose darting flames escaped through the curls of the most beautiful golden hair in the world, were quite touching at that moment. They had that charm better felt perhaps in France than anywhere else: they revealed a soul which has been thought frozen for years past and which all of a sudden becomes animated, but for you, and for you _alone_. The electrical effect produced in Madame de Bonnivet by this instant of perfect beauty and the natural tone full of feeling which it imparted to her accents made her truly seductive. At that moment, she would have gone to the scaffold to assure the triumph of her new religion; generosity and devotion shone in her eyes. What a triumph for the malice that was watching her. And these two people, the most remarkable in the room, in which, all unconsciously, they were providing a spectacle, had no thought of their own pleasure; nothing was farther from their minds. This is what would have seemed perfectly incredible to Madame la Duchesse d'Ancre and her neighbours, the most refined women in France. Thus it is that matters of sentiment are judged in society.

Armance had remained perfectly consistent in her attitude towards her cousin. Several months had passed without her addressing a word to him upon personal matters. Often she did not speak to him throughout an evening, and Octave was beginning to note the days upon which she had deigned to be aware of his presence.

Being careful not to appear disconcerted by Mademoiselle de Zohiloff's hatred, Octave was no longer remarkable in society for his invincible silence nor for the singular and perfectly noble air with which, in the past, those fine eyes of his had seemed to shew their boredom. He talked freely and without the least regard for the absurdities into which he might be led. In this way he became, unconsciously, one of the most fashionable of the male visitors to the drawing-rooms which in a sense were dependent upon Madame de Bonnivet's. He was indebted to the perfect want of interest with which he approached everything for a real superiority over his rivals; he arrived without pretensions among a crowd of people who were devoured by them. His _fame_, descending from the drawing-room of the illustrious Marquise de Bonnivet into social spheres in which that lady was envied, had placed him without the least effort in a most agreeable position. Without having as yet done anything, he saw himself, from his first entry into society, classed as a being apart. There was nothing about him, not even the disdainful silence with which he was at once inspired by the presence of people whom he thought incapable of understanding exalted feelings, that was not accepted as a striking singularity.

Mademoiselle de Zohiloff observed this success and was amazed by it. In the last three months, Octave was no longer the same man. It was not surprising that his conversation, so brilliant to every one else, had a secret charm for Armance; the sole object of that conversation was to give her pleasure.

Towards midwinter, Armance thought that Octave was going to make a brilliant marriage, and it was easy to estimate the social position to which a few months had sufficed to raise the young Vicomte de Malivert. There appeared now and again in Madame de Bonnivet's drawing-room a very great nobleman indeed who had all his life been on the watch for things or people that were going to become the fashion. His mania was to attach himself to these, and to this strange idea he was indebted for a considerable social success; a man of the commonest mould, he had raised himself far above his level. This great nobleman, as servile towards Ministers as any clerk, was on the best of terms with them, and he had a grand-daughter, his sole heir, to whose husband he would be able to convey the highest honours and the greatest benefits that it is in the power of the Monarchy to bestow. All this winter he had appeared to have his eye upon Octave, but no one as yet dreamed of the heights to which the young Vicomte was to rise. M. le Duc de--------was giving a great stag-hunt in his forests in Normandy. To be admitted to these parties was a distinction; and for the last thirty years he had not issued an invitation for which skilful commentators could not divine a reason.

Suddenly, and without a word of warning, he wrote a charming note to the Vicomte de Malivert, inviting him to come and hunt with him. It was decided in Octave's family circle, perfectly acquainted with the ways and character of the old Duc de-------, that if his visit to the Château de Ranville should prove a success, they would one day see him a Duke and a Peer of France. He set off loaded with good advice by the Commander and the rest of the household; he had the honour to see a stag and four excellent hounds fling themselves into the Seine from a rock one hundred feet high, and on the third day he was back in Paris.

"You are evidently mad," Madame de Bonnivet said to him before Armance. "Does the young lady displease you?" "I scarcely examined her," he replied with great coolness, "she seems to me quite pleasant; but when the hour struck at which I-always come here I felt my soul plunged in darkness."

The religious discussions waxed warmer than ever after this fine piece of philosophy. Octave seemed to Madame de Bonnivet an astonishing creature. At length, the instinct of the conventions, if I dare venture upon such an expression, or certain intercepted smiles gave the fair Marquise to understand that a drawing-room in which one hundred persons assemble every evening is not precisely the most appropriate place in the world in which to _investigate rebellion_.
She told Octave one evening to come to the house next day at noon, after breakfast. This was an invitation for which Octave had long been waiting.
The day following was one of the most brilliant of the month of April. The presence of spring in the air was revealed by a delicious breeze and gusts of warmth. Madame de Bonnivet decided to transport her theological conference into the garden. She was confident of finding in the _always novel_ spectacle of nature some striking argument in support of one of the fundamental ideas of her philosophy: "_What is really beautiful must always be true_." The Marquise had indeed been talking extremely well and for a considerable time, when a maid came in search of her to remind her to pay her respects to a foreign Princess. This was an engagement which she had made a week earlier; but the interest of the new religion, of which it was hoped that Octave would one day be the Saint Paul, had banished every other thought from her mind. As the Marquise felt herself in the mood for discussion, she asked Octave to wait for her. "Armance will keep you company," she added.
As soon as Madame de Bonnivet had left them: "Do you know, cousin, what my _conscience_ tells me?" Octave went on at once without the least timidity, for timidity is begotten of the love that knows itself and makes pretensions; "It tells me that for the last three months you have been despising me as a vulgar fellow whose head has been absolutely turned by the hope of an increase of fortune. I have long sought to justify myself to you, not by vain words but by actions. I can think of none that would be decisive; I, too, can have recourse only to your _intimate sense_, Well, this is what has happened to me. While I am talking, look in my eyes and see whether I am lying." And Octave began to relate to his young kinswoman, with great wealth of detail and with the most perfect simplicity, the whole sequence of sentiments and endeavours of which the reader has been informed. He did not forget the speech addressed by Armance to her friend Méry de Tersan, which he had overheard when going to fetch the Chinese

chessmen. "Those words determined the course of my life; from that moment I have thought of nothing but how to regain your esteem." This memory touched Armance deeply, and silent tears began to trickle down her cheeks.

She did not once interrupt Octave; when he had finished speaking, she still remained silent for a long time. "You think me guilty!" said Octave, extremely touched by this silence. She did not answer. "I have forfeited your esteem," he cried, and the tears trembled on his eyelids. "Tell me of any single action in the world by which I can reconquer the place I once held in your heart, and in an instant it will be performed." These last words, uttered with a restrained and deep-rooted energy, were too much for Armance's courage to endure; it was no longer possible for her to pretend, her tears overpowered her, and she wept openly. She was afraid lest Octave might go on and say something that would increase her discomfiture, and make her lose what little self-control she still retained. Above all, she was afraid to speak. She made haste to offer him her hand; and making an effort to speak, and to speak only as a friend: "You have all my esteem," she told him. She was greatly relieved to see a maid approaching in the distance; the necessity of concealing her tears from the girl furnished her with an excuse for leaving the garden.

CHAPTER SEVEN

_But passion most dissembles, yet betrays
Even by its darkness; as the blackest sky
Foretells the heaviest tempest, it displays
Its workings through the vainly guarded eye,
And in whatever aspect it arrays
Itself,'tis still the same hypocrisy;
Coldness or anger, even disdain or hate,
Are masks it often wears, and still too late._
   DON JUAN, I, 73.

Octave remained motionless, his eyes brimming with tears, and not
knowing whether he ought to rejoice or to mourn. After so long a
period of waiting, he had at last been able to give battle, that
battle for which he had so longed; but had he lost or won it? "If it
is lost," he told himself, "there is nothing more for me in this
direction. Armance thinks me so reprehensible that she pretends to be
satisfied with the first excuse that I offer her, and does not deign
to enter upon an explanation with a man so little worthy of her
friendship. What is the meaning of those brief words: _You have all my
esteem_? Could anything be colder? Is that a complete return to our
old intimacy? Is it a polite way of cutting short a disagreeable
explanation?" The departure, so abruptly, of Armance seemed to him to
be an especially evil omen.

While Octave, a prey to a profound astonishment, was seeking to recall
exactly what had happened to him, trying to forecast the consequences,
and trembling lest, amid his efforts to reason fairly, he should
suddenly arrive at some decisive revelation which would make an end of
all uncertainty by proving to him that his cousin found him unworthy
of her esteem, Armance was being racked by the most intense grief. Her
tears choked her; but they were tears of shame and no longer of
happiness.

She hastened to shut herself up in her own room. "Great God," she
said to herself in the intensity of her confusion, "what on earth will
Octave think after seeing me in this state? Has he understood my
tears? Alas! Can I doubt it? Since when has a simple admission of
friendship made a girl of my age burst into tears? Oh, God! After such
humiliation how can I venture to face him again? The only thing
wanting to complete the horror of my situation was to have deserved

his contempt. But," Armance said to herself, "it was something more than a simple admission; for three months I avoided speaking to him; it is a sort of reconciliation between friends who have quarrelled, and people say that one sheds tears at reconciliations of that sort;--yes, but one does not run away, one is not plunged in the most intense confusion.

"Instead of shutting myself up and crying in my bedroom, I ought to be out in the garden and to go on talking to him, happy in the simple happiness of friendship. Yes," Armance told herself, "I ought to go back to the garden; perhaps Madame de Bonnivet has not yet returned." As she rose, she looked at herself in the glass and saw that she was not in a fit state to let herself be seen by a man. "Ah!" she cried, letting herself sink down in despair upon a chair, "I am a poor wretch who has forfeited her honour, and in whose eyes? In Octave's." Her sobs and her despair prevented her from thinking.

"What!" she said to herself, after an interval, "so peaceful, so happy even, in spite of my fatal secret, half an hour ago, and now ruined! Ruined for ever, without remedy! A man of such intelligence as his must have seen the whole extent of my weakness, and it is one of the weaknesses that must be most offensive to his stern judgment." Armance was stifled by her tears. This violent state continued for some hours; it produced a slight touch of fever which won for Armance the permission not to leave her room that evening.

The fever increased, presently an idea came to her: "I am only half despicable, for after all I did not confess in so many words my fatal secret. But after what has happened, I cannot answer for anything. I must erect an eternal barrier between Octave and myself. I must enter religion, I shall choose the order that allows most solitude, a convent situated among high mountains, with a picturesque view. There I shall never hear his name spoken. This is the voice of _duty_," the unhappy Armance told herself. From that moment the sacrifice was made. She did not say it to herself, she felt (to express it in detail would have been tantamount to doubting it), she felt this truth: "From the moment when I perceived my _duty_, not to follow it immediately, blindly, without argument, is to act in a vulgar spirit, is to be unworthy of Octave. How often has he told me that this is the secret sign by which one can recognise a noble spirit! Ah! I will submit to your decree, my noble friend, my dear Octave!" Her fever emboldened her to utter his name in a whisper, and she found happiness in repeating it.

Presently Armance was picturing herself as a nun. There were moments in which she was astonished at the mundane ornaments which decorated her little room. "That fine engraving of the Sistine Madonna which Madame de Malivert gave me, I too must give it away," she said to herself; "it was chosen by Octave, he preferred it to the Marriage of the Madonna, Raphael's first painting. Even then I remember that I argued with him over the soundness of his choice, solely that I might have the pleasure of hearing him defend it. Was I in love with him then without knowing it? Have I always loved him? Ah! I must tear that dishonourable passion from my heart." And the unhappy Armance, trying to forget her cousin, found his memory blended with all the events of her life, even the most insignificant. She was alone, she had sent her maid away, to be able to weep without constraint. She rang the bell and had her engravings carried into the next room. Soon the little room was stripped bare and adorned only with its pretty wallpaper of a lapis-lazuli blue. "Is a nun allowed," she wondered, "to have a wallpaper in her cell?" She pondered for long over this difficulty; her spirit needed to form an exact idea of the state to which she would be reduced in her cell; her uncertainty in this matter surpassed all other evils, for it was her imagination that was engaged in portraying them. "No," she said to herself at length, "papers cannot be allowed, they were not invented in the days of the foundresses of the religious orders; these orders come from Italy; Prince Touboskin told us that a white wall, washed every year with lime, is the only ornament of many beautiful monasteries. Ah!" she went on in her delirium, "I ought perhaps to go and take the veil in Italy; I should make my health an excuse.
"Oh, no. Let me at least not leave Octave's native land, let me at least always hear his tongue spoken." At this moment Méry de Tersan entered the room; the bareness of the walls caught her eye; she turned pale as she approached her friend. Armance, exalted by her fever and by a certain virtuous enthusiasm which was also another way of being in love with Octave, sought to bind her by a confidence. "I wish to become a nun," she said to Méry. "What! Has the sereness of a certain person's heart gone so far as to wound your delicacy?" "Oh, Lord, no, I have no fault to find with Madame de Bonnivet; she is as fond of me as she can be of a penniless girl who has no position in society. Indeed, she is loving to me when things vex her, and could not be kinder to any one than she is to me. I should be unjust, and be shewing a spirit worthy of my position, if I reproached her in the

slightest degree." One of the final phrases of this reply drew tears
from Méry, who was rich and had the noble sentiments that distinguish
her illustrious family. Without conversing save by their tears and the
pressure of one another's hand, the friends spent a great part of the
evening together. Finally, Armance told Méry all her reasons for
retiring to a convent, with one exception: what was to become socially
of a penniless girl, who after all could not be given in marriage to a
small shopkeeper round the corner? What fate was in store for her? In
a convent one is bound only by the rule. If there are not those
distractions which we owe to the arts and to the intelligence of
people in society, distractions which she enjoyed with Madame de
Bonnivet, there is never either the absolute necessity of attracting
one person in particular, with humiliation if one does not succeed.
Armance would have died of shame sooner than utter the name of Octave.
"This is the climax of my misery," she thought, weeping and throwing
herself into Méry's arms. "I cannot ask advice even of the most
devoted, the most virtuous friendship."
While Armance was weeping in her room, Octave, yielding to an impulse
which, for all his philosophy, he was far from explaining to himself,
knowing that throughout the evening he would not set eyes on
Mademoiselle de Zohiloff, engaged in talk with the women whom as a
rule he neglected for the religious argument's of Madame de Bonnivet.
For many months now Octave had found himself pursued by advances which
were extremely polite and all the more irritating in consequence. He
had become misanthropical and soured; soured like Alceste, on the
subject of marriageable daughters. As soon as any one spoke to him of
a woman in society whom he did not know, his first remark was: "Has
she a daughter to marry?" Latterly, indeed, his prudence had taught
him not to be satisfied with an initial reply in the negative. "Madame
So-and-So has no daughter to marry," he would say, "but are you sure
there isn't some niece or other?"
While Armance was being racked by delirium, Octave, who was seeking
distraction from the uncertainty in which the incident of the
afternoon had plunged him, not only talked to all the women who had
nieces, but even tackled several of those redoubtable mothers who have
as many as three daughters. Perhaps this display of courage had been
rendered easy to him by the sight of the little chair on which Armance
generally sat, near Madame de Bonnivet's armchair; it had just been
taken by one of the young ladies de Claix, whose fine German
shoulders, benefiting by the lowness of Armance's little seat, took

the opportunity to display all their freshness. "What a difference!" thought or rather felt Octave; "how ashamed my cousin would be of what constitutes the triumph of Mademoiselle de Claix! For her, it is no more than permissible coquetry; it is not even a fault; of this, too, one can say: _Noblesse oblige_." Octave set to work to pay court to Mademoiselle de Claix. It would have required some personal motive for trying to understand him or greater familiarity with the habitual simplicity of his expression to detect all the bitterness and scorn that underlay his pretended gaiety. His listeners were kind enough to discover wit in what he said to them; to himself the remarks that received most applause seemed quite commonplace and sometimes even tainted with vulgarity.

As he had not once stopped to talk to Madame de Bonnivet during the evening, when she passed by him she scolded him in a whisper, and Octave apologised for his desertion of her in a speech which the Marquise thought charming. She was highly pleased with the intelligence of her future proselyte, and the self-possessed air which he assumed in society.

She sang his praises with the artless candour of innocence (if the word _candour_ does not blush to see itself employed with reference to a woman who could adopt such charming poses in her _bergère_ and whose eyes were so picturesque when raised to heaven). It must be confessed that at times, when she gazed fixedly at a gilded ornament on the ceiling of her drawing-room, she would actually say to herself: "There, in that empty space, in that air, there is a Spirit who hears me, magnetises my soul and imparts to it the singular and really quite spontaneous sentiments which I express at times with such eloquence." That evening, Madame de Bonnivet, highly pleased with Octave and with the thought of the position to which her disciple might one day rise, said to Madame de Claix: "Indeed, the only thing wanting to the young Vicomte was the assurance that is given by wealth. Even if I were not in love with that excellent Law of Indemnity, because it is so fair to our poor _emigres_, I should love it for the new spirit it has given my cousin." Madame d'Ancre shot a glance at Madame de Claix and Madame la Comtesse de la Ronze; and as Madame de Bonnivet left these ladies, in order to greet a young Duchesse who was entering the room: "It seems to me to be all quite clear," she said to Madame de Claix. "All too clear," the latter replied: "we shall be having a scandal; only a little more friendliness on the part of the _astounding_ Octave, and our dear Marquise will be unable to resist the temptation to take us altogether into her confidence."

"That is always the way," went on Madame d'Ancre, "that I have seen these people of pronounced virtue end, who go in for laying down the law about religion. Ah! my dear Mai'quise, blessed is the woman who just listens meekly to her parish priest and offers the holy bread!"

"It is certainly better than having Bibles bound by Thouvenin," put in Madame de Claix. But all Octave's feigned friendliness had vanished in the twinkling of an eye. He had just caught sight of Méry, who had come down from Armance's bedroom because her mother had sent for her carriage, and Méry's face was woebegone. She left so hurriedly that Octave had no opportunity of speaking to her. He himself left immediately after her. It would have been impossible for him from that moment to address a word to any one. The distressed air of Mademoiselle de Tersan told him that something out of the common was happening; perhaps Mademoiselle de Zohiloff was about to leave Paris to escape him. What is truly remarkable is that our philosopher had not the slightest idea that he was genuinely in love with Armance. He had bound himself by the strongest vows to resist that passion, and as what he lacked was penetration rather than character, he would probably have kept his vows.

CHAPTER EIGHT

What shall I do the while? where bide? how live?
Or in my life what comfort, when I am
Dead to him?
   CYMBELINE, Act III.

Armance was far from being under any such illusion. It was now a long
time since to see Octave had become her one interest in life. When an
unexpected turn of fortune had altered her young kinsman's position in
society, how her heart had been torn by inward conflicts! What excuses
had she not invented for the sudden change that had become apparent in
Octave's behaviour! She asked herself incessantly: "Has he a vulgar
soul?"

When at length she had succeeded in proving to herself that Octave was
capable of feeling other forms of happiness than those arising from
money and vanity, a fresh cause of distress seized her attention. "I
should be doubly scorned," she said to herself, "were any one to
suspect my feelings for him; I, the most penniless of all the girls
who come to Madame de Bon-nivet's drawing-room." This utter misery
which threatened her from every side, and which ought to have set her
to curing herself of her passion, had no effect, but, by inducing in
her a profound melancholy, that of abandoning her more blindly than
ever to the sole pleasure that remained to her in the world, the
pleasure of thinking of Octave.

Every day she saw him for some hours, and the petty incidents of each
day affected her mental attitude towards her cousin; how could she
possibly be cured? It was from fear of betraying herself and not from
scorn that she had taken such good care never to have any intimate
conversation with him.

On the day following the explanation in the garden, Octave called
twice at the Hôtel de Bonnivet, but Armance did not appear. This
strange absence greatly increased his uneasiness as to the favourable
or disastrous effect of the step he had ventured to take. That
evening, he read his sentence in his cousin's absence and had not the
heart to seek distraction in the sound of vain words; he could not
bring himself to speak to any one.

Whenever the door of the drawing-room opened, he felt that he was
about to die of hope and fear combined; at length one o'clock struck,
and it was time to go. As he left the Hôtel de Bonnivet, the hall, the

street-front, the black marble lintel of the door, the crumbling wall of the garden, all these things, common enough in themselves, seemed to him to wear a new and special aspect, derived from Armance's anger. Their familiar forms became precious to Octave, owing to the melancholy which they inspired in him. Dare I say that they rapidly acquired in his eyes a sort of tender nobility? He shuddered when next day he detected a resemblance between the old wall of his father's garden, crowned with a few yellow wall-flowers in blossom, and the enclosing wall of the Hôtel de Bonnivet.

On the third day after his venturing to speak to his cousin, he called upon the Marquise, firmly convinced that he had been for ever relegated to the category of mere acquaintance. What was his dismay on, catching sight of Armance at the piano? She greeted him in a friendly fashion. He thought her pale and greatly altered. And yet--and this astonished him greatly and almost restored a glimpse of hope--he thought he could detect in her eyes a certain trace of happiness.

The weather was perfect, and Madame de Bonnivet wished to take advantage of one of the most beautiful mornings of spring to make some long excursion. "Will you be one of us, cousin?" she said to Octave. "Yes, Madame, if it is not to be the Bois de Boulogne, nor the Bois de Mousseaux." Octave knew that Armance disliked both places. "The King's Garden, if we go by the boulevard; will that find favour in your sight?" "It is more than a year since I was last there." "I have never seen the baby elephant," said Armance, jumping for joy, as she went to put on her hat. They set off gaily. Octave was almost beside himself; Madame de Bonnivet drove along the boulevard in an open carriage with her good-looking Octave, This was how the men of their circle who saw them spoke of them. Those whose livers were out of order gave utterance to melancholy reflexions as to the frivolity of great ladies, who were reverting to the ways of the Court of Louis XV. "In the serious events towards which we are marching," these poor creatures went on to say, "it is a great mistake to let the Third Estate and the working classes have the advantage of regularity of morals and decent behaviour. The Jesuits are perfectly right to make a point of severity."

Armance said that her aunt's bookseller had just sent three volumes entitled _History of-----_. "Do you recommend the book?" the Marquise asked Octave. "It is so blatantly praised in the newspapers that I am distrustful of it." "You will find it very well written, all the

same," Octave told her; "the author knows how to tell a story and he has not yet sold himself to any party." "But is it amusing?" said Armance. "Plaguily dull," replied Octave. The talk turned to historical certainty, then to monuments. "Did you not tell me, the other day," said Madame de Bonnivet, "that there is nothing certain except ancient monuments?" "Yes, for the history of the Romans and Greeks, who were rich people and built monuments; but the libraries contain thousands of manuscripts dealing with the middle ages, and it is only from pure laziness on the part of our so-called scholars that we do not make use of them." "But those manuscripts are written in such vile Latin," Madame de Bonnivet went on. "Barely intelligible perhaps to our scholars, but not so bad. You would be highly pleased with the Letters of Heloise to Abelard." "Their tomb used to be, I have heard, in the Musée Français,"said Armance,"what has become of it?" "It has been set up in Père-Lachaise." "Let us go and look at it," said Madame de Bonnivet, and a few minutes later they arrived in that English garden, the only garden of real beauty as a site that exists in Paris. They visited the tomb of Abelard, the obelisk erected to Masséna; they looked for the grave of Labédoyère. Octave saw the spot where rests the young B------, and made her an oblation of tears. Their conversation was serious, grave, but touching in its intensity. Their true feelings came boldly to the surface. As a matter of fact, they touched only upon subjects that were hardly likely to compromise them, but the heavenly charm of candour was none the less keenly felt by the party, when they saw advancing upon them a group the presiding deity of which was the clever Comtesse de G------. She came to the place in search of inspiration, she informed Madame de Bonnivet. At this speech, our friends could barely help smiling; never had the commonness and affectation that underlay the words seemed to them so shocking. Madame de G------, like all vulgar French people, exaggerated her impressions in order to create an effect, and the people whose conversation she was interrupting modified their sentiments slightly when they expressed them, not from insincerity but from a sort of instinctive modesty which is unknown among common people, however intelligent they may be.
After a few words of general conversation, as the path was extremely narrow, Octave and Armance found themselves left in the rear.
"You were unwell the day before yesterday," said Octave; "indeed, your friend Méry's pallor, when she came down from your room, made me afraid that you must be feeling very ill."

"I was not ill at all," said Armance in a tone the lightness of which
was a trifle marked, "and the interest which your old friendship takes
in all that concerns me, to speak like Madame de G------, makes it my
duty to tell you the cause of my little disturbance. •For some time
past there has been a question of my marriage; the day before
yesterday, it was on the point of being broken off, and that is why I
was a little upset in the garden. But I beg of you absolute secrecy,"
said Armance in alarm as Madame de Bonnivet began to move towards
them. "I rely upon eternal secrecy, even from your mother, and
especially from my aunt." This avowal greatly astonished Octave;
Madame de Bonnivet having again withdrawn: "Will you permit me to ask
one question," he went on. "Is it purely a marriage of convenience?"
Armance, to whose cheeks the fresh air and exercise had brought the
most vivid colours, suddenly turned pale. When forming her heroic
project overnight, she had not foreseen this very simple question.
Octave saw that he had been indiscreet, and was trying to think of
some way of turning the conversation with a jest, when Armance said to
him, making an effort to subdue her grief: "I hope that the person in
question will deserve your friendship; he has all mine. But, if you
please, let us not say any more about this arrangement, which is still
perhaps far from complete." Shortly afterwards, they returned to the
carriage, and Octave, who could think of nothing more to say, asked to
be set down at the Gymnase.

CHAPTER NINE

Now, peace be here,
Poor house, that keep'st thyself!
CYMBELINE, Act III.
[Footnote: Beyle ascribes this motto, which he quotes in French, to
Burns, thinking possibly of various phrases in the lines _To a Field
House_. In _Henri Brulard_ he again quotes the passage, as from
Cymbeline, but gives the speech to Imogen instead of Belarius.--C.
K. S. M.]

On the evening before this, after a terrible day of--which we can at
the most form a feeble idea by thinking of the state of a poor wretch
wholly devoid of courage who is preparing to undergo a surgical
operation that often proves fatal, an idea had occurred to Armance: "I
am on sufficiently intimate terms with Octave to tell him that an old
friend of my family is thinking of marrying me. If my tears betrayed
me, this confession will re-establish me in his esteem. My approaching
marriage and the anxiety it must be causing me, will make him set my
tears down to some allusion a trifle too direct to the position in
which I am placed. If he takes any interest in me, alas! he will be
cured of it, but at least I can still be his friend; I shall not be
banished to a convent and condemned never to set eyes on him again,
never once even, for the rest of my life."

Armance realised, during the days that followed, that Octave was
seeking to discover who the favoured suitor might be, "It will have to
be some one whom he knows," she said to herself with a sigh; "my
painful duty extends to that also. It is only on those terms that I
may still be permitted to see him."

She thought of the Baron de Risset, who had been a leader in the
Vendée, a heroic character, who appeared not infrequently in Madame de
Bonnivet's drawing-room, but only to remain silent.

The very next evening, Armance spoke to the Baron of the _Memoirs_ of
Madame de Rochejaquelein. She knew that he was jealous of their
success; he spoke of them very critically and at great length. "Is
Mademoiselle de Zohiloff in love with a nephew of the Baron," Octave
asked himself, "or can it be possible that the old General's gallant
deeds have made her forget his fifty-five years?" It was in vain that
Octave tried to draw the taciturn Baron, who was more silent and
suspicious than ever now that he saw himself made the object of these

singular attentions.

Some pieces of politeness unduly marked, addressed to Octave by a mother of marriageable daughters, aroused his misanthropy and made him say to his cousin, who was praising the young ladies in question, that even although they had a more eloquent sponsor, he had, thank God, forbidden himself all exclusive admiration until he should reach the age of six and twenty. This unexpected utterance came like a bolt from the blue to Armance; never in all her life had she felt so happy. Ten times perhaps since his change of fortune, Octave had spoken in her hearing of the time at which he would think of marrying. From the surprise which her cousin's words caused her, she realised that she had forgotten all about it.

This moment of happiness was exquisite. Wholly absorbed the day before in the intense pain that is caused by a great sacrifice which must be made to duty, Armance had entirely forgotten this admirable source of comfort. It was forgetfulness of this sort which made her be accused of want of intelligence by those people in society whom the emotions of their hearts leave with the leisure to think of everything. As Octave was just twenty, Armance might hope to be his best friend for six years still, and to be so _without remorse_. "And who knows," she said to herself, "but I may have the good fortune to die before the end of those six years?"

A new mode of existence began for Octave. Authorised by the confidence which Armance placed in him, he ventured to consult her as to the petty incidents of his life. Almost every evening he had the happiness of being able to talk to her without being actually overheard by the people near them. He observed with delight that his confidences, however trivial they might be, were never burdensome. To give courage to her diffidence, Armance too spoke to him of her troubles, and a very singular intimacy sprang up between them.

The most blissful love has its storms; one may even say that it lives as much by its terrors as by its felicities. Neither storms nor any uneasiness ever disturbed the friendship of Armance and Octave. He felt that he had no claim upon his cousin; there was nothing that he could have complained of.

Far from exaggerating the gravity of their relations, these delicate natures had never uttered a word on the subject; the word friendship even had never been spoken by either since the confession of her proposed marriage, made by the tomb of Abelard. As, though they met continually, they were rarely able to converse without being overheard, they had always in their brief moments of entire freedom so many things to learn, so many facts to communicate rapidly to one another, that all vain delicacy was banished from their speech.

It must be admitted that Octave would have had difficulty in finding grounds for complaint. All the sentiments that the most exalted, the tenderest, the purest love can bring to life in a woman's heart, Armance felt for him. The hope of death, in which the whole prospect of that love terminated, gave indeed to her speech something heavenly and resigned, quite in keeping with Octave's character.

The tranquil and perfect happiness with which Armance's gentle affection filled him, was felt by him so keenly that he hoped to change his own nature.

Since he had made peace with his cousin, he had never again relapsed into moments of despair, as when he regretted that he had not been killed by the carriage which turned at a gallop into the Rue de Bourbon. He said to his mother: "I am beginning to think that I shall no longer have those fits of rage which made you fear for my reason." Octave was happier, and became more intelligent. He was astonished to notice in society many things which had never before struck him, though they had long been before his eyes. The world seemed to him less hateful, and, above all, less intent upon doing him harm. He told himself that, except among the class of pious or plain women, everybody thought far more about himself, and far less about doing harm to his neighbour, than he had supposed at a time when he imagined a world which he did not yet know.

He realised that an incessant frivolity makes any consecutive reasoning impossible; he discovered at last that this world, which, in his insensate pride, he had believed to be arranged in a manner hostile to himself, was simply nothing more than ill arranged. "But," he said to Armance, "such as it is, one must take it or leave it. One must either end everything swiftly and without delay with a few drops of prussic acid, or else take life gaily." In speaking thus, Octave was trying to convince himself far more than he was expressing a conviction. His heart was beguiled by the happiness that he owed to Armance.

His confidences were not always free from peril for the girl. When Octave's reflexions took on a sombre hue; when he was made wretched by the prospect of isolation in time to come, Armance had the greatest difficulty in concealing from him how wretched it would have made her to imagine that she might ever for an instant in her life be parted from him.

"When a man is without friends at my age," Octave said to her one evening, "can he still hope to acquire Does one love according to plan?" Armance, who felt that her tears were about to betray her, was obliged to leave him abruptly. "I see," she said to him, "that my aunt wishes to speak to me."

Octave, his face pressed to the window, continued by himself the course of his sombre reflexions. "It does not do to scowl at the world," he said to himself at length. "It is so spiteful that it would not deign to notice that a young man, shut up under lock and key on a second floor in the Rue Saint-Dominique, hates it with passion. Alas! One creature alone would notice that I was missing from my place, and her _friendship_ would be distressed"; and he began to gaze across the room at Armance; she was sitting on her little chair beside the Marquise, and seemed to him at that moment ravishingly beautiful. All Octave's happiness, which he imagined to be so solid and so well assured, depended nevertheless upon the one little word _friendship_ which he had just uttered. It is difficult to escape from the prevailing disease of one's generation: Octave imagined himself to be philosophical and profound.

Suddenly Mademoiselle de Zohiloff came towards him with an air of uneasiness and almost of anger: "My aunt has just been told," she said to him, "a strange slander at your expense. A serious person, who has never before shewn himself your enemy, came and told her that often at midnight, when you leave this house, you go and end the evening in strange places which are nothing more than gambling rooms.

"And that is not all; in these places, in which the most degrading tone prevails, you distinguish yourself by excesses which astonish their oldest frequenters. Not only are you seen surrounded by women the mere sight of whom is a scandal; but you talk, you hold the ball in their conversation. She went so far as to say that you shine in those places, and by pleasantries, the bad taste of which passes all belief. The people who take an interest in you, for there are such to be found even in those houses, did you the honour at first to take your utterances for _acquired_ wit. 'The Vicomte de Malivert is young,' they said to themselves; 'he must have heard these pleasantries used at some vulgar gathering to stimulate attention and make pleasure sparkle in the eyes of a few coarse men.' But your friends have observed with pain that you take the trouble to invent your most revolting speeches for the occasion. In short, the incredible scandal of your alleged conduct seems to have earned you an unfortunate celebrity among the young men of the worst tone that are to be found in Paris.

"The person who slanders you," continued Armance, whom Octave's obstinate silence was beginning somewhat to disconcert, "ended by giving details which only my aunt's astonishment prevented her from contradicting."

Octave observed with delight that Armance's voice began to tremble during this long speech. "Everything that you have been told is true," he said to her at length, "but it shall never happen again. I will not appear any more in those places in which your friend ought never to have been seen."

Armance's astonishment and distress were intense. For an instant she felt a sentiment akin to contempt. But next day, when she saw Octave again, her attitude towards what is fitting in the conduct of a young man had quite altered. She found in her cousin's noble confession, and still more in that simple promise made to herself, a reason for loving him all the more. Armance thought that she was being sufficiently severe with herself when she made a vow to leave Paris and never to see Octave again, should he reappear in those houses that were so unworthy of him.

CHAPTER TEN

_O conoscenza-t non è senna il suo perché
ché il fedel prête ti chiamo: il più gran dei mali.
Egli era tutto disturbato, e pero non dubi-tava ancora,
al più al più, dubitava di esser presto sul punto
di dubitare. O conoscenza! tu sei fatale a quelli, nei quali
l'oprar segue da vicino il credo_.
  IL CARDINAL GERDIL.

Need it be said that Octave was faithful to his promise? He abandoned
the pleasures proscribed by Armance.

The need for action and the desire to acquire novel experiences had
driven him to frequent bad company, often less tedious than good. Now
that he was happy, a sort of instinct led him to mix with men; he
wished to dominate them.

For the first time, Octave had caught a glimpse of the tedium of too
perfect manners and of the excess of cold politeness: bad tone allows
a man to talk about himself, in and out of season, and he feels less
isolated. After punch had been served in those brilliant saloons at
the end of the Rue de Richelieu, which foreigners mistake for good
company, one no longer has the sensation: "I am alone in a wilderness
of people." On the contrary, he can imagine that he has a score of
intimate friends, whose names are unknown to him. May we venture to
say, at the risk of compromising at one and the same time both our
hero and ourself: Octave thought with regret of several of his supper
companions.

The part of his life that had elapsed before his intimacy with the
inhabitants of the Hôtel de Bonnivet was beginning to strike him as
foolish and marred by misunderstanding. "It rained," he would say to
himself in his original and vivid manner; "instead of taking an
umbrella, I used foolishly to lose my temper with the state of the
sky, and in moments of enthusiasm for what was beautiful and right,
which were after all nothing but fits of madness, I used to imagine
that the rain was falling on purpose to do me an ill turn."

Charmed with the possibility of talking to Mademoiselle de Zohiloff of
the observations he had made, like a second Philibert, in certain
highly elegant ballrooms: "I found it a little unexpected," he would
say to her. "I no longer find such pleasure in that preeminently good
society, of which I was once so fond. It seems to me that beneath a

cloak of clever talk it proscribes all energy, all originality. If you are not a copy, people accuse you of being ill-mannered. And besides, good society usurps its privileges. It had in the past the privilege of judging what was proper, but now that it supposes itself to be attacked, it condemns not what is coarse and disagreeable without compensation, but what it thinks harmful to its interests."

Armance listened coldly to her cousin, and said to him finally: "From what you think to-day, it is only a step to Jacobinism." "I should be in despair," Octave sharply retorted. "In despair at what? At knowing the truth," said Armance. "For obviously you would not let yourself be converted by a doctrine that was marred by falsehood." Throughout the rest of the evening, Octave could not help seeming lost in meditation. Now that he saw society in a rather truer light, Octave was beginning to suspect that Madame de Bon-nivet, for all her supreme pretension of never thinking about the world and of despising success, was the slave of an ambition which made her long for an unbounded success in society.

Certain calumnies uttered by the Marquise's enemies, which chance had brought to his hearing, and which had seemed to him unspeakably horrible a few months earlier, were now nothing more in his eyes than exaggerations, treacherous or in bad taste. "My fair cousin is not satisfied," he said to himself, "with illustrious birth, an immense fortune. The splendid existence which her irreproachable conduct, her prudent mind, her wise benevolence assure her is perhaps only a means to her and not an end.

"Madame de Bonnivet requires power. But she is very particular as to the nature of that power. The respect which one obtains from a great position in society, from a welcome at court, from all the advantages that are to be enjoyed under a monarchy no longer means anything to her, she has enjoyed it too long. When one is King, what more can one want? To be God.

"She is satiated with the pleasure that comes from calculated respect, she needs a respect from the heart. She requires the sensation which Mahomet feels when he talks to Seïde, and it seems to me that I have come very near to the honour of being Seide. [Footnote: A slave of Mahomet in Voltaire's tragedy.]

"My fair cousin cannot fill her life with the sensibility that she lacks. She needs, not touching or sublime illusions, not the devotion and passion of one man alone, but to see herself regarded as a Prophetess by a crowd of initiates, and above all, if one of them

rebels, to be able to crush him immediately. She has too positive a
nature to be content with illusions; she requires the reality of
power, and, if I continue to talk to her with an open heart about
various things, one day that absolute power may be brought into action
against me.

"It is inevitable that she must soon be besieged by anonymous letters;
people will reproach her with the frequency of my visits. The Duchesse
d'Ancre, irritated by my neglect of her own drawing-room, will perhaps
allow herself to make a direct charge. My position is not strong
enough to withstand this twofold danger. Very soon, while scrupulously
maintaining all the outward forms of the closest friendship, and
heaping reproaches on me for the infrequency of my visits, Madame de
Bonnivet would put me under the obligation to make them very
infrequent indeed.

"For instance, I give the impression of being half converted to this
German mysticism; she will ask me to make some public and utterly
ridiculous exhibition. If I submit to that, out of friendship for
Armance, very soon she will suggest to me something that is quite
impossible."

CHAPTER ELEVEN

_Somewhat light as air.
There's language in her eye, her cheek, her lip,
Nay, her foot speaks; her wanton spirits look out
At every joint and motive of her body.
O! These encounterers, so glib of tongue,
That give a coasting welcome ere it comes._
    TROILUS AND CRESSIDA, Act IV.
[Footnote: The first half-line, which is not in _Troilus and
Cressida_, is perhaps a reminiscence of _Othello_: "Trifles light as
air."-- C. K. S. M.]

There were few pleasant drawing-rooms pertaining to that section of
society which three times in the year pays its respects to the King in
which Octave was not warmly welcomed. He observed the celebrity of
Madame la Comtesse d'Aumale. She was the most brilliant and perhaps
the cleverest coquette of the day. An ill-humoured foreigner has said
that the women of high society in France have a cleverness akin to
that of an old Ambassador. It was a childish simplicity that shone in
the manners of Madame d'Aumale. The artlessness of her repartees and
the wild gaiety of her actions, always inspired by the circumstances
of the moment, were the despair of her rivals. She had caprices of a
marvellous unexpectedness, and how is any one to imitate a caprice?
The natural and unexpected were by no means the most brilliant element
in Octave's behaviour. He was compact of mystery. Never any sign of
thoughtlessness in him, unless occasionally in his conversations with
Armance. But he needed to be certain that he would not be interrupted
unexpectedly. No one could reproach him with falseness; he would have
scorned to tell a lie, but he never went straight towards his goal.
Octave took into his service a footman who had come from Madame
d'Aumale; this man, an old soldier, was ambitious and cunning. Octave
used to make him ride with him on long excursions of seven or eight
leagues which he made through the forests round Paris, and there were
moments of evident boredom in which the man was allowed to talk. It
was barely a matter of weeks before Octave had the most definite
information as to Madame d'Aumale's conduct. This young woman, who had
compromised herself deeply by an unbounded thoughtlessness, was really
entitled to all the esteem which certain people no longer gave her.
Octave calculated, pencil in hand, the amount of time and trouble

which Madame d'Aumale's society would require of him, and hoped, without undue effort, to be able before long to pass as a lover of this brilliant woman. He arranged matters so well that it was Madame de Bonnivet herself who, in the course of a party that she was giving at her country house at Andilly, presented him to Madame d'Aumale, and the manner of the presentation was picturesque and impressive for the giddy young Comtesse.

With the object of enlivening a stroll that the party were taking, by night, among the charming woods that crown the height» of Andilly, Octave suddenly appeared disguised as a magician, and was seen in a glare of Bengal lights, cunningly concealed behind the trunks of forest trees. Octave was looking his best that evening, and Madame de Bonnivet, quite unconsciously, spoke of him with a sort of exaltation. Less than a month after this first encounter, people began to say that the Vicomte had succeeded M. de R-------and all the rest of them in the post of intimate friend to Madame d'Aumale.

This most frivolous of women, of whom neither she herself nor any one else could ever say what she would be doing in a quarter of an hour, had noticed that a drawing-room clock, when it struck twelve, sent home the majority of the bores in the room, people of regular habits; and so entertained from midnight until two o'clock. Octave was always the last to leave Madame de Bonnivet's drawing-room, and would kill his horses to hasten his arrival at Madame d'Aumale's, in the Chaussée d'Antin. There he found a woman who thanked heaven for her exalted birth and her fortune, solely because of the privilege they conferred on her, to do at every minute of the day whatever she might be inspired to do by the caprice of the moment.

In the country, at midnight, when every one went up to bed, did Madame d'Aumale remark, as she crossed the hall, a fine night and a pleasing moon, she would take the arm of the young man who, that evening, seemed to her to be the most amusing, and go roaming through the woods. Should some fool offer to accompany her on her stroll, she would beg him without ceremony to choose another path; but next day, should her companion overnight have proved boring, she did not speak to him again. It must be confessed that in the presence of so lively an intelligence, employed in the service of so unbalanced a head, it was very difficult not to seem a trifle dull.

This was what made Octave's fortune; the amusing element of his nature was completely invisible to the people who before taking action always think of a. model to be copied and of the conventions. No one, on the other hand, could be more conscious of this than the prettiest woman in Paris, always in pursuit of some novel idea which might enable her to pass the evening in an exciting way. Octave accompanied Madame d'Aumale everywhere, as for instance to the Italian theatre.

During the two or three final performances given by Madame Pasta, to which the cult of fashion had brought the whole of Paris, he took the trouble to converse aloud with the young Comtesse, and in such a way as to spoil the whole of the show. Madame d'Aumale, amused by what he was saying to her, was delighted by the simple air with which he displayed his impertinence.

Nothing could have seemed in worse taste to Octave; but he was beginning to acquire a mastery of foolish conduct. The twofold attention which, when he took some ridiculous liberty, he gave unconsciously to the impertinence that he was committing and to the sober conduct for which he substituted it, kindled a certain fire in his eyes which, amused Madame d'Aumale. Octave took pleasure in hearing it said on all sides that he was madly in love with the Comtesse, and in never saying anything to this young and charming woman, with whom he spent all his time, that in the remotest degree suggested love.

Madame de Malivert, astonished at her son's conduct, went now and again to the drawing-rooms in which he was to be seen in the train of Madame d'Aumale. One evening, as she left Madame de Bonnivet's, she asked her to let her have Armance for the whole of the next day. "I have a number of papers to arrange, and I need the eyes of my Armance."

On the following morning, at eleven o'clock, before luncheon, as had been arranged, Madame de Malivert's carriage went to fetch Armance: The ladies took luncheon by themselves. When Madame de Malivert's maid was leaving them, "remember," her mistress told her, "that I am at home to nobody, neither to Octave nor to M. de Malivert." She carried her precautions so far as to bolt the door of her outer room herself. When she was comfortably settled in her _bergère_, with Armance on her little chair facing her: "My child," she said to her, "I am going to speak to you of a matter which I have long ago decided. But unfortunately my most firm desire is not enough to bring about a result which would be the joy of my life. You have but a hundred louis a year, that is all that my enemies can say against the passionate desire that I fee! to make you marry my son." So saying, Madame de Malivert threw herself into Armance's arms. This was the happiest moment in the poor girl's life; tears of joy bathed her cheeks.

CHAPTER TWELVE

_Estamas, linda Ignez, posta em socego
De teus annos colhendo doce fruto
Naquelle engano da alma ledo e cego
Que a fortuna; naô deixa durar muito.
OS LUSIADAS, III.

"But, dear Mama," said Armance, after a long pause, and when they were once more able to talk seriously, "Octave has never told me that he was attached to me as it seems to me that a husband ought to be to his wife." "If I had not to rise from my chair to take you in front of a mirror," replied Madame de Malivert, "I should let you see how your eyes are sparkling with joy at this moment, and should ask you to repeat to me that you are not sure of Octave's heart. I am quite sure of it myself, though I am only his mother. However, I am under no illusion as to the faults that my son may have, and I do not ask for your answer before at least a week has passed." I cannot say whether it was to the Slavonic blood that flowed in her veins, or to her early experience of misfortune that Armance owed her faculty of perceiving in a flash all the consequences that a sudden change in her life might involve. And whether this new state of things were deciding her own fate or that of some one to whom she was indifferent, she saw the outcome with the same clarity of vision. This strength of character or of mind entitled her at once to the daily confidences and to the reprimands of Madame de Bonnivet.

The Marquise consulted her readily as to her own most private arrangements; and at other times would say to her: "A mind like yours is never becoming in a girl."

After the first moment of happiness and profound gratitude, Armance decided that she ought not to say anything to Madame de Malivert of the untrue statement she had made to Octave with regard to a proposal of marriage. "Madame de Malivert has not consulted her son," she thought, "or else he has concealed from her the obstacle in the way of his plan." This second possibility made Armance extremely sombre. She wished to believe that Octave felt no love for her; every day she had need of this certainty to justify in her own eyes any number of attentions which her tender affection allowed her to pay him, and yet this terrible proof of her cousin's indifference, which came to her thus suddenly, crushed her heart under an enormous weight, and deprived her of the power of speech.

With what sacrifices would not Armance have paid at that moment for the right to weep freely! "If my cousin surprises a tear in my eyes," she said to herself, "what decisive conclusion will she not feel herself entitled to draw from it? For all I can tell, in her eagerness for this marriage, she may mention my tears to her son, as a proof of my response to his supposed affection." Madame de Malivert was not at all surprised at the air of profound abstraction which dominated Armance at the end of this day.

The ladies returned together to the Hôtel de Bonnivet, and although Armance had not set eyes on her cousin all day, even his presence, when she caught sight of him in the drawing-room, was powerless to wrest her from her black melancholy. She could barely answer him; she had not the strength to speak. Her preoccupation was plain to Octave, no less than her indifference towards him; he said to her sadly: "To-day you have not time to remember that I am your friend." Armance's only answer was to gaze at him fixedly, and her eyes assumed, unconsciously, that serious and profound expression which had earned her such fine moral lectures from her aunt.

These words from Octave pierced her to the heart. "So he knows nothing of his mother's intervention, or rather he took no interest in it, and wished only to be a friend." When, after seeing the guests depart and receiving Madame de Bonnivet's confidences as to the state of all her various plans, Armance was at length able to seek the solitude of her little room, she found herself a prey to the most sombre grief. Never had she felt so wretched; never had the act of living so hurt her. With what bitterness did she reproach herself for the novels among whose pages she sometimes allowed her imagination to stray! In those happy moments, she ventured to say to herself: "If I had been born to a fortune, and Octave could have chosen me as his companion in life; according to what I know of his character, he would have found greater happiness with me than with any other woman in the world."

She was paying dearly now for these dangerous suppositions. Armance's profound grief did not grow any less in the days that followed; she could not abandon herself for a moment to meditation, without arriving at the most entire disgust with everything, and she had the misfortune to feel her state keenly. The external obstacles in the way of a marriage to which, upon any assumption, she would never have consented, seemed to be smoothed away; but Octave's heart alone was not on her side.

Madame de Malivert, having seen the dawn of her son's passion for Armance, had been alarmed by his assiduous courtship of the brilliant Comtesse d'Aumale. But she had only had to see them together to discern that this relation was a duty which her son's odd nature had imposed on him; Madame de Malivert knew quite well that if she questioned him on the subject, he would tell her the truth; but she had carefully abstained from asking even the most indirect questions. Her rights did not seem to her to extend so far. Out of regard for what she thought due to the dignity of her sex, she had wished to speak of this marriage to Armance before opening the subject with her son, of whose passion she was sure.

Having disclosed her plan to Mademoiselle de Zohiloff, Madame de Malivert arranged her time so that she spent hours on end in Madame de Bonnivet's drawing-room. She thought she could see that something strange was occurring between Armance and her son. Armance was evidently very unhappy. "Can it be possible," Madame de Malivert asked herself, "that Octave, who adores her and sees her incessantly, has never told her that he is in love with her?"

The day upon which Mademoiselle de Zohiloff was to give her answer had arrived. Early in the morning Madame de Malivert sent round her carriage with a little note in which she invited her to come and spend an hour with her. Armance arrived with the face of a person who is recovering from a long illness; she would not have had the strength to come on foot. As soon as she was alone with Madame de Malivert, she said to her in the gentlest of tones, beneath which could be seen that firmness which comes of despair: "My cousin has a strain of originality in his character; his happiness requires, and perhaps mine also," she added, blushing deeply, "that my darling Mama shall never speak to him of a plan which her extreme interest in myself has inspired in her." Madame de Malivert affected to grant with great reluctance her consent to what was asked of her. "I may die Sooner than I think," she said to Armance, "and then my son will never win the only woman in the world who can mitigate the despondency of his nature. I am sure that it is the thought of money that has led to your decision," she said at other moments; "Octave, who has always something to confide in you, cannot have been such a fool as not to confess to you a thing of which I am certain, namely, that he loves you with all the passion of which he is capable, which is saying a great deal, my child. If certain moments of excitement, which become rarer every year, may furnish grounds for sundry objections to the character of the husband I offer you, you will have the comfort of being loved as few women are loved to-day. In the stormy times that may come upon us, firmness of character in a man will mean a great probability of happiness for his family.

"You yourself know, my Armance, that the external obstacles which crush down common men are nothing to Octave. If his soul is at peace, the whole world banded together against him would not give him a quarter of an hour of unhappiness. Well, I am certain that the peace of his soul hangs upon your consent. Judge for yourself of the ardour with which I ought to plead for him; on you depends my son's happiness. For four years I thought day and night of how to assure it, I could find no way; at last he fell in love with you. As for myself, I shall be the victim of your exaggerated delicacy. You do not wish to incur the reproach of having married a husband far richer than yourself, and I shall die with the utmost anxiety as to Octave's future, and without having seen my son united to the woman whom, in my whole life, I have most highly esteemed."

These assurances of Octave's love were excruciating to Armance. Madame de Malivert remarked, underlying her young relative's answers, irritation and wounded pride. That evening, at Madame de Bonnivet's, she observed that her son's presence did not at all relieve Mademoisele de Zohiloff of that sort of misery which springs from the fear of not having shewn sufficient pride towards the person whom one loves, and of having perhaps thus lowered herself in his esteem. "Is a poor girl with no family," Armance was saying to herself, "the person to be so forgetful?"

Madame de Malivert herself was extremely anxious. After many sleepless nights, she at length arrived at a curious idea, probable however in view of her son's strange character, that really, just as Armance had said, he had never uttered a word to her of his love.

"Is it possible," thought Madame de Malivert, "that Octave can be so timid as that? He is in love with his cousin; she is the one person in the world who can ensure him against those fits of melancholy which have made me tremble for him."

After careful reflexion, she decided upon her course; one day she said to Armance in an indifferent tone: "I cannot think what you have done to my son, to discourage him; but while he admits to me that he has the most profound attachment to you, the most entire esteem, and that to win your hand would be in his eyes the greatest of blessings, he adds that you present an insuperable obstacle to his most cherished ambitions, and that certainly he would not be indebted for you to the persecutions to which we might subject you on his behalf."

CHAPTER THIRTEEN

_Ay! que ya siento en mi cuidoso pecho
Labrarme poco a poco un vivo fuego
Y desde alli con movimiento blando
Ir par venas y huesos penetrando_.
  ARAUCANA, XXII.

The extreme happiness that shone in Armance's eyes consoled Madame de
Malivert, who was beginning to feel some remorse at having introduced
a tiny falsehood into so serious a negotiation. "After all," she said
to herself, "what harm can there be in hastening the marriage of two
charming but rather proud children, who feel a passion for each other
such as we rarely see in this world? To preserve my son's reason, is
not that my paramount duty?"

The singular course which Madame de Malivert had decided to adopt had
delivered Armance from the most profound grief that she had ever felt
in her life. A little while since, she had longed for death; and now
these words, which she supposed to have been uttered by Octave, placed
her on a pinnacle of happiness. She was quite determined never to
accept her cousin's hand; but this charming speech allowed her once
again to nope for many years of happiness. "I shall be able to love
him in secret," she told herself, "during the six years that must pass
before he marries; and I shall be fully as happy, and perhaps far
happier than if I were his partner. Is it not said that marriage is
the grave of love; that there may be agreeable marriages but never one
that is really delightful? I should be terrified of marrying my
cousin; if I did not see that he was the happiest of men, I should
myself be in the depths of despair. If, on the other hand, we continue
to live in our pure and holy friendship, none of the petty concerns of
life can ever reach the high level of our feelings to wound them."

Armance weighed in her mind with all the calm of happiness the reasons
which she had given herself in the past for never accepting Octave's
hand. "I should be regarded in society as a paid companion who had
seduced the son of the house. I can hear Madame la Duchesse d'Ancre
saying so, and indeed the most honourable women, such as the Marquise
de Seyssins, who looks on Octave as a husband for one of her
daughters.

"The loss of my reputation would be all the more rapid, from my having
lived in the company of several of the most unimpeachable women in

Paris. They can say anything they like about me; their word will be believed. Heavens! Into what an abyss of shame they can hurl me! And Octave might at any time withdraw his esteem from me; for I have no means of defence. What drawing-room is there in which I could make my voice heard? Where are my friends? And besides, after the evident baseness of such an action, what justification would be possible? Even if I had a family, a brother, a father, would they ever believe that, if Octave was in my position and I extremely rich, I should be as devoted to him as I am at this moment?"

Armance had a reason for feeling keenly the kind of indelicacy which money involves. Only a few days earlier, Octave had said to her, speaking of a certain majority vote which had made a stir: "I hope, when I have taken my place in public life, that I shall not allow myself to be bought like those gentlemen. I can live upon five francs a day; and, under an assumed name, it is open to me to earn twice that amount in any part of the world, as a chemist employed in some factory."

Armance was so happy that she did not shrink from examining any objection, however perilous it might be to discuss it. "If Octave preferred me to a fortune and to the support which he is entitled to expect from the family of a wife of his own rank, we might go and live somewhere in retirement. Why not spend ten months of every year on that charming estate Malivert, in Dauphiné, of which he often speaks? The world would very soon forget us.--Yes; but I myself, I should not forget that there was a place on earth where I was despised, and despised by the noblest souls.

"To see love perish in the heart of a husband whom she adores is the greatest of all misfortunes for a young person born to wealth; well, that terrible misfortune fould be as nothing to me. Even if he continued to cherish me, every day would be poisoned by the fear that Octave might come to think that I had chosen him because of the difference in our fortunes. That idea will not come to him spontaneously, I am sure; anonymous letters, like those that are sent to Madame de Bonnivet, will bring it to his notice. I shall tremble at every mail that he receives. No, whatever happens, I must never accept Octave's hand; and the course that honour prescribes is also the most certain to assure our happiness."

On the morrow of the day that made Armance so happy, Mesdames de Malivert and de Bonnivet went to stay in the charming house that the Marquise owned near Andilly. Madame de Malivert's doctors had

recommended exercise on horseback and on foot; and on the morning
after her arrival she decided to try a pair of charming little ponies
which she had procured from Scotland for Armance and herself. Octave
accompanied the ladies on their first ride. They had scarcely gone a
quarter of a league before he thought he noticed a slight increase of
reserve in his cousin's attitude towards himself, and especially a
marked tendency to gaiety.

This discovery gave him much food for thought; and what he observed
during the rest of the ride confirmed his suspicions. Armance was no
longer the same to him. It was clear that she was going to be married;
he was going to lose the only friend that he had in the world. As he
was helping Armance to dismount, he found an opportunity to say to
her, without being overheard by Madame de Malivert: "I am sorely
afraid that my fair cousin is soon going to change her name; that
event will deprive me of the only person in the world who has been
kind enough to shew me some friendship." "NEVER," said Armance, "will
I cease to feel for you the most devoted and most exclusive
friendship." But while she was rapidly uttering these words, there was
such a look of happiness in her eyes, that Octave, forewarned, saw in
them the confirmation of all his fears.

The good nature, the air almost of intimacy with which Armance treated
him during their ride on the following day, succeeded in robbing him
of all peace of mind: "I see," he said to himself, "a decided change
in Mademoiselle de Zohiloff's manner; she was extremely agitated a few
days ago, now she is extremely happy. I am ignorant of the cause of
this change; therefore it can only be to my disadvantage.

"Who was ever such a fool as to choose for his intimate friend of a
girl of eighteen? She marries, and all is over. It is my cursed pride
that makes me prepared to die a thousand deaths rather than venture to
say to a man the things that I confide in Mademoiselle de Zohiloff.

"Work might offer some resource; but have I not abandoned every
reasonable occupation? To tell the truth, for the last six months, has
not the effort to make myself agreeable in the eyes of a stupid and
selfish world been my only task?" So as to devote himself at any rate
to this useful form of boredom, every day, after his mother's outing,
Octave left Andilly and went to pay calls in Paris. He sought new
habits to fill the void that would be left in his life by this
charming cousin when she withdrew from society to go with her husband;
this idea put him in need of violent exercise.

The more his heart was wrung by misery, the more he spoke and sought to please; what he most feared, was finding himself left alone; and, above all, the prospect of the future. He repeated incessantly to himself: "It was childish of me to choose a girl as my friend." This statement, by its self-evident truth, soon became a sort of proverb in his eyes, and prevented him from proceeding farther with his exploration of his own heart.

Armance, who saw his misery, was moved by it, and often reproached herself for the false admission she had made to him. Not a day passed but, as she saw him set off for Paris, she was tempted to tell him the truth. "But that falsehood is my one weapon against him," she said to herself; "if I so much as admit to him that I am not engaged, he will implore me to yield to his mother's wishes, and how am I to resist? And yet, never and upon no pretext must I consent; no, this pretended marriage with a stranger is my sole defence against a happiness that would destroy us both."

To dissipate the sombre thoughts of this beloved cousin, Armance allowed herself to indulge in the little pleasantries of the most tender friendship. There was such charm, such an artless gaiety in the assurances of undying friendship given him by this girl, so natural in all her actions, that often Octave's dark misanthropy was disarmed by them. He was happy in spite of himself; and at such moments nothing was wanting either to complete Armance's happiness.

"How pleasant it is," she said to herself, "to do one's duty! If I were Octave's wife, I, a penniless girl with no family, should I be as well pleased? A thousand cruel suspicions would assail me without ceasing." But, after these moments in which she was satisfied with herself and with the rest of the world, Armance ended by treating Octave more kindly than she intended. She kept a careful watch over her speech; and never did her speech convey anything but the most holy friendship. But the tone in which certain words were uttered! The glance that sometimes accompanied them! Any one but Octave would have been able to read in them an expression of the warmest passion. He enjoyed without understanding them.

As soon as he had granted himself permission to think incessantly of his cousin, his thoughts no longer rested with passion upon anything else in the world. He became once more fair and even indulgent; and his happiness made him abandon his harsh judgments of many things: fools no longer seemed to him anything more than people who had been unlucky from birth.

"Is it a man's fault if he has black hair?" he said to Armance. "But it rests with me carefully to avoid the man if the colour of his hair annoys me."

Octave was considered malicious in certain sections of society, and fools had an instinctive fear of him; at this period they became reconciled with him. Often he took with him into society all the happiness that he owed to his cousin. He was less feared, his affability was felt to be more youthful. It must be admitted that in all his actions there was a trace of that intoxication which springs from that form of happiness which a man does not admit even to himself; life passed rapidly for him and delightfully. His criticisms of himself no longer bore the imprint of that inexorable, harsh logic, taking pleasure in its own harshness, which in his boyhood had controlled all his actions. Beginning often to speak without knowing how his sentence would end. he talked far better than before.

CHAPTER FOURTEEN

_Il giovin cuore o non vede affatto i difetti
di chi li sta vicino o li vede immensi.
Error comune ai giovinetti che portano fuoco nell'
interna dell' anima.
LAMPUGNANI.

One day Octave learned in Paris that one of the men whom he saw most
often and took most pleasure in seeing, one of his friends, as the
word is used in society, owed the handsome fortune which he spent with
such grace to what in Octave's eyes was the basest of actions (legacy
hunting). Mademoiselle de Zohiloff, to whom he made haste, immediately
on his return to Andilly, to impart this painful discovery, felt that
he bore it very well. He underwent no attack of misanthropy, shewed no
desire to quarrel openly with the man.

Another day, he returned quite early from a country house in Picardy,
where he was to have spent the evening. "How dull all that talk is!"
he said to Armance. "Always hunting, the beauty of the country,
Rossini's music, the fine arts! Not only that, but they are lying when
they pretend to be interested. These people are foolish enough to be
frightened, they imagine they are living in a beleaguered city and
forbid themselves to discuss the news of the siege. What a miserable
race! And how angry it makes me to belong to it!" "Very well! Go and
visit the besiegers," said Armance; "their absurdities will help you
to endure those of the army in which your birth has enrolled you." "It
is a serious question," Octave went on. "Heaven knows what I feel when
I hear in one of our drawing-rooms one of our friends give voice to
some opinion that is absurd or cruel; still, I can remain honourably
silent. My regret remains invisible. But if I let myself be taken to
see the banker Martigny..." "There you are," said Armance, "a man so
refined as he is, so clever, such a slave to his vanity, will receive
you with open arms." "Doubtless; but for my part, however moderate,
however modest, however silent I try to make myself, I shall end by
expressing my opinion about somebody or something. A moment later, the
door of the drawing-room is flung open; the butler announces Monsieur
So-and-so, manufacturer at-------, who in stentorian tones shouts from
the threshold: 'Would you believe it, my dear Martigny, there are
ultras, fools enough, stupid enough, idiotic enough to say that...'
Whereupon the worthy manufacturer repeats, word for word, the little

scrap of opinion which I have just announced in all modesty. What am I
to do?" "Pretend not to have heard him." "That is what I should like.
I was not put into this world to correct coarse manners or wrong
judgments; still less do I wish to give the man, by speaking to him,
the right to shake hands with me in the street when next we meet. But
in that drawing-room I have the misfortune not to be just like any one
else. Would to God that I might find there the _equality_ of which all
those gentlemen make so much. For instance, what would you have me do
with the title that I bear when I am announced at M. de Martigny's?"
"But it is your intention to discard the title if you can manage to do
so without offending your father." "Doubtless; but to forget the
title, in giving my name to M. de Martigny's servant, might seem,
might it not, an act of cowardice? Like Rousseau, who called his dog
Turc instead of _Duc_, because there was a Duke in the room."
[Footnote: Like Rousseau, poor Octave is fighting against phantoms.
He would have passed unnoticed in any drawing-room in Paris,
notwithstanding the prefix to his name. There prevails, moreover, in
his sketch of a section of society which he has never seen, an absurd
tone of animosity which he will correct in time. Fools are to be
found in every class. If there were a class which rightly or wrongly
was accused of coarseness, it would very soon be distinguished by a
great prudery and solemnity of manners.]
"But there is no such hatred of titles among the Liberal bankers,"
said Armance. "The other day Madame de Claix, who goes everywhere,
happened to go to the ball at M. Montange's, and you remember how she
made us laugh that evening by pretending that they are so fond of
titles that she had heard some one announced as 'Madame la
Colonelle.'"
"Now that the steam engine rules the world, a title is an absurdity,
still I am dressed up in this title. It will crush me if I do not
support it. The title attracts attention to myself. If I do not reply
to the thundering voice of the manufacturer who shouts from the door
that what I have just said is asinine, how they will all stare at me.
That is the weak point in my nature: I cannot simply twitch my ears
and laugh at them, as Madame d'Aumale would suggest.
"If I intercept their stare, all my pleasure is gone for the rest of
the evening. The discussion that will then begin in my mind, as to
whether they meant to insult me, is capable of destroying my peace of
mind for three days."
"But are you quite certain," said Armance, "of this alleged coarseness

of manners which you so generously attribute to the other side? Did not you see the other day that Talma's children are boarding at the same school as the sons of a Duke?" "It is the men of forty-five, who became rich during the Revolution, who hold the ball in our drawing-rooms, not the schoolfellows of Talma's children." "I would wager that they have more intelligence than many of us. Who is the man who shines in the House of Peers? You yourself made that painful observation the other day."

"Oh! If I were to give my fair cousin lessons in logic, how I should tease her! What is a man's intelligence to me? It is his manners that may make me unhappy. The most foolish of our men, M. de-------, for instance, may be highly ridiculous, but he is never offensive. The other day I was talking at the Aumales' of my visit to Liancourt; I was talking of the latest machinery which the worthy Duke has imported from Manchester. A man who was in the room said suddenly: 'It's not so, that's not true.' I was quite sure that he did not mean to contradict me; but his rudeness kept me silent for an hour."

"And this man was a banker?" "He was not one of us. The amusing thing is, that I wrote to the foreman of the mills at Liancourt, and it appears that my friend who contradicted me was quite wrong." "I don't find that M. Montange, the young banker who comes to see Madame de Claix, has rude manners." "His are honeyed; it is a form that rude manners take, when they are frightened."

"I think their women very pretty," Armance went on. "I should like to know whether their conversation is marred by that note of hatred or of dignity that is afraid of being wounded, which appears at times among us. Oh, how I wish that a good judge like my cousin could tell me what goes on in those drawing-rooms! When I see the bankers' ladies in their boxes, at the Théâtre-Italien, I am dying with longing to hear what they say and to join in their conversation. If I catch sight of a pretty one, and some of them are charming, I long to throw my arms round her neck. All this will seem childish to you; but to you, master philosopher, who are so strong in logic, I will say this: how are you to know mankind if you see only one class? And the class that is least energetic because it is the farthest removed from any real needs!"

"And the class that has most affectation, because it thinks that people are watching it. You must admit that it is amusing to see a philosopher supply his adversary with arguments," said Octave, laughing. "Would you believe that yesterday, at the Saint-Imiers', M. le Marquis de-------, who, the other day, in this house, made such fun

of the little newspapers, and pretended not to know of their
existence, was in the seventh heaven, because _l'Aurore_ had printed a
vulgar joke about his enemy, M. le Comte de-------, who has just been
made a Privy Councillor? He had the paper in his pocket.""It is one of
the drawbacks of our position, to have to listen to fools telling the
most ridiculous lies and not be able to say: 'A fine disguise, I know
you.'" "We are obliged to deny ourselves the best jokes, because they
might make the other side laugh if they heard them."

"I know the bankers," said Armance, "only from our silvery Montange
and that charming comedy _Le Roman_; but I doubt whether, as far as
the worship of money is concerned, they are any worse than some of our
own people. You know that it is a hard task to maintain the perfection
of a whole class. I shall say no more of the pleasure it would give me
to know more about their ladies. But, as the old Duc de--------said at
Petersburg, when he had the _Journal de l'Empire_ sent to him at such
expense, and at the risk of offending the Tsar Alexander: 'Ought one
not to read what the other side has to say?'" "I will go a great deal
farther, _but in confidence_, as Talma says so perfectly in
Polyeucte: You and I, in our hearts, do not, certainly, wish to live
among these people; but on many questions we think as they do." "And
it is sad at our age," Armance put in, "to have to resign ourselves to
being for the rest of our lives on the defeated side."

"We are like the priests of the heathen idols, at the time when the
Christian religion was beginning to triumph. We still persecute
to-day, we still have the police and the budget on our side, but
to-morrow, perhaps, we shall be persecuted by public opinion." "You do
us a great honour when you compare us to those worthy priests of
paganism. I see something even more false in our position, yours and
mine. We belong to our party only to share its misfortunes." "That is
all too true, we see its absurdities without daring to laugh at them,
and its advantages are a burden to us. How does the antiquity of my
name help me? It would be a nuisance to me to derive any benefit from
that advantage."

"The conversation of the young men of your sort makes you sometimes
want to shrug your shoulders, and, afraid of yielding to the
temptation, you are always in a hurry to speak of Mademoiselle de
Claix's beautiful album or of Madame Pasta's singing. On the other
hand, your title and the manners, which are slightly rough perhaps, of
the people who think like you on most questions prevent you from
seeing them."

"Ah, how I should love to command a gun or a steam engine! How glad I should be to be a chemist employed in some factory; for rude manners are nothing to me, one grows accustomed to them in a week." "Apart from the fact that you are by no means so certain that they are so rude," said Armance. "Were they ten times more so," replied Octave, "there is the excitement of trying a foreign language; but one would have to be called M. Martin or M. Lenoir." "Could you not find a man of sense who had made a tour of discovery in the Liberal drawing-rooms?" "Many of my friends go there to dance, they say that the ices there are perfect, and that is all. One fine day I may venture there myself, for there is nothing so foolish as to think for a year on end of a danger which perhaps does not exist."

In the end, Armance extracted the admission that he had thought of a way of appearing in those circles in which it is wealth that confers precedence and not birth: "Well, yes, I have found a way," said Octave; "but the remedy would be worse than the disease, for it would cost me several months of my life, which I should have to spend away from Paris."

"What is your way?" said Armance, growing suddenly quite serious. "I should go to London, I should see there, naturally, all the most distinguished elements of society. How can one go to England and not be introduced to the Marquess of Lansdowne, Mr. Brougham, Lord Holland? These gentlemen will talk to me of our famous men in France; they will be surprised to hear that I do not know them; I shall express deep regret; and, on my return, I shall have myself introduced to all the most popular people in France. My action, if they do me the honour to mention it at the Duchesse d'Ancre's, will not seem in the least an abandonment of the ideas which they may suppose to be inseparable from my name: it would be simply the quite natural desire to know the superior people of the age in which we live. I shall never forgive myself for not having met General Foy." Armance remained silent.

"Is it not humiliating," Octave went on, "that all our supporters, even the _monarchist_ writers whose duty it is to preach every morning in the newspaper the advantages of birth and religion, are furnished us by that class which has every advantage, except that of birth?" "Ah, if M. de Soubirane were to hear you!" "Do not attack me upon the greatest of all my misfortunes, that of being obliged to lie all day long...."

The tone of perfect intimacy allows endless parentheses, which give pleasure because they are a proof of an unbounded confidence, but may easily bore a third person. It is enough for us to have shewn that the brilliant position of the Vicomte de Malivert was far from being a source of unmixed pleasure to him.

It is not without danger that we have been faithful chroniclers. The intrusion of politics into so simple a narrative may have the effect of a pistol shot in the middle of a concert. Moreover, Octave is no philosopher, and has characterised most unfairly the two shades of opinion which, in his day, bisect society. How scandalous that Octave does not reason like a sage of fifty.

[Footnote: We are not sufficiently grateful to the Villèle Ministry. The Three Per Cents, the Law of Primogeniture, the Press Laws have brought about a fusion of parties. The inevitable relations between the Peers and the Deputies began this reconciliation which Octave could not have foreseen, and fortunately the ideas of this proud and timid young man are even less true to-day than they were a few months ago; but this is how he was bound to see things, given his character. Must we leave unfinished the sketch of an eccentric character because he is unfair to every one? It is precisely this unfairness that is his misfortune.]

CHAPTER FIFTEEN

_How am I glutted with conceit of this!
Shall I make spirits fetch me what I please,
Resolve me of all ambiguities,
Perform what desperate enterprise I will?
    DOCTOR FAUSTUS.

Octave was so much in the habit of leaving Andilly to visit Madame
d'Aumale in Paris, that one day a slight feeling of jealousy began to
quench Armance's gaiety. On her cousin's return, that evening, she
exercised her authority. "Do you wish to oblige your mother in a
matter which she will never mention to you?" "Of course." "Very well,
for the next three months, that is to say for ninety days, do not
refuse any invitation to a ball, and do not come away from a ball
until you have danced."

"I should prefer a fortnight's imprisonment." "You are easily
satisfied," Armance went on, "but do you promise me, or do you not?"
"I promise anything except to keep my promise for three months. Since
you all tyrannise over me here," said Octave with a laugh, "I shall
run away. There is an old idea of mine which quite spontaneously kept
coming into my mind throughout the evening yesterday, at M.
de-------'s sumptuous party, at which I danced as though I had guessed
your orders. If I were to leave Andilly for six months I have two
plans more amusing than that of going to England.

"One is to assume the name of M. Lenoir; under that fine name, I
should go into the country and give lessons in arithmetic, in geometry
applied to the arts, anything they want to learn. I should make my way
by Bourges, Aurillac, Cahors; I should easily procure letters from any
number of Peers who are Members of the Institute, recommending to the
Prefects the learned royalist Lenoir, and so forth.

"But the other plan is better still. In my capacity as a teacher, I
should see only a lot of enthusiastic and volatile young fellows who
would soon bore me, and various intrigues by the _Congregation_.

"I hesitate to reveal to you the better plan of the two; I should
assume the name of Pierre Gerlat, I should start at Geneva or Lyons by
becoming valet to some young man who is destined to play a part more
or less identical with my own in society. Pierre Gerlat would be
provided with excellent testimonials from the young Vicomte de
Malivert, whose faithful servant he had been for six years. In a word,

I should assume the name and identity of that poor Pierre whom I once threw out of the window. Two or three men of my acquaintance will oblige me with testimonials. They will seal these with their arms upon huge lumps of wax, and in that way I hope to find a place with some young Englishman, either very rich or the son of a Peer. I shall take care to stain my hands with an acid solution. I have learned how to clean boots from the servant I have now, the gallant Corporal Voreppe. In the last three months I have stolen all his talents."

"One evening your roaster, when he comes home tipsy, will start kicking Pierre Gerlat."

"Were he to throw me out of the window, I am prepared for that. I shall defend myself, and give him notice the next day, and bear him no grudge whatever."

"You would be guilty of an abuse of confidence which would be very wrong indeed; A man exposes the defects of his nature to a young peasant who is incapable of understanding his most salient eccentricities, but he would take good care, I am sure, not to act thus before a man of his own class." "I shall never repeat what I have seen or heard. Anyhow, a master, to talk like Pierre Gerlat, always runs the risk of hitting upon a rascal, mine will only find curiosity. Realise what I am suffering," Octave went on. "My imagination is so foolish at certain moments, and so far exaggerates what I owe to my position, that, without being a Sovereign Prince, I long for an incognito. I am supreme in misery, in absurdity, in the extreme importance that I attach to certain things. I feel a compelling need to see another Vicomte de Malivert in my place. Since, unfortunately, I have embarked on this career, since, to my great and sincere regret, I cannot be the son of the chief foreman of M. de Lian-court's carding mill, I require six months of domestic service to cure the Vicomte de Malivert of various weaknesses.

"This is the only way; my pride raises a wall of adamant between myself and my fellow men. Your presence, my dear cousin, makes this unsurmountable wall disappear. In conversation with you, I should take nothing in ill part, such serenity does your presence give to my soul, but unfortunately I have not the magic carpet to take you everywhere with me. I cannot see you as a third person when I go riding in the Bois de Boulogne with one of my _friends_. Soon after our first meeting, there is none of them who is not _estranged_ by my talk. When, after a year, and in spite of anything I can do, they understand me thoroughly, they wrap themselves up in the closest reserve, and would rather (I really believe) that their secret thoughts and actions were known to the devil than to me. I would not swear that many of them do not take me for _Lucifer himself_ (as M. de Soubirane says, in fact, it is one of his favourite remarks) _brought into the world on purpose to torment them_."

Octave imparted these strange ideas to his cousin as they strolled in the woods of Moulignon, in the wake of Mesdames de Bonnivet and de Malivert. These oddities distressed Armance deeply. Next day, after her cousin had left for Paris, her free and lively air which often became quite unrestrained gave way to that fixed and tender gaze from which Octave, when he was present, could not tear his own.

Madame de Bonnivet invited a number of guests, and Octave no longer had such frequent reasons for going to Paris, for Madame d'Aumale came to stay at An-dilly. With her there arrived seven or eight women at the height of the fashion, and mostly remarkable for the brilliance of their wit or for the influence that they had obtained in society. But their affability only enhanced the triumph of the charming Comtesse; her mere presence in a drawing-room aged her rivals.

Octave was too intelligent not to feel this, and Armance's spells of musing became more frequent. "Of whom have I the right to complain?" she asked herself. "Of no one, and of Octave least of all. Have I not told him that I prefer another man? And there is too much pride in his nature to be content with the second place in a heart. He is attached to Madame d'Aumale; she is a brilliant beauty, spoken of everywhere, and I am not even pretty. Anything that I can say to Octave can be but faintly interesting, I am certain that often I bore him, or am interesting only as a sister. Madame d'Aumale's life is gay, unusual; things never flag where she is to be found, and it seems to me that I should often be bored in my aunt's drawing-room if I listened to what people say there." Armance wept, but her noble soul did not so far debase itself as to feel hatred for Madame d'Aumale. She observed every action of that charming lady with a profound attention which ended often in moments of keen admiration. But each act of admiration was like a dagger thrust in her heart. Her peaceful happiness vanished, Armance was a prey to all the anguish of the passions. Finally, Madame d'Aumale's presence disturbed her more than that of Octave himself. The torture of jealousy is most unbearable when it is rending hearts to which their natural inclination as well as their social position forbid every way of appeal that is at all dangerous.

CHAPTER SIXTEEN

_Let Rome in Tiber melt, and the wide arch
Of the rang'd empire fall! Here is my space.
Kingdoms are clay; our dungy earth alike
Feeds beast as man: the nobleness of life
Is to love thus.
　　ANTONY AND CLEOPATRA, Act I.

One evening after a day of stifling heat, they were strolling quietly
amid the handsome groves of chestnuts that crown the heights of
Andilly. Sometimes during the day these woods are spoiled by the
intrusion of strangers. On this charming night, bathed in the calm
light of a summer moon, these deserted slopes were an enchantment to
the eye. They assumed a certain grandeur, the dark shadows cast by a
brilliant moon eliminated their details. A soft breeze was playing
among the trees, and completed the charms of this delicious evening.
>From some caprice or other, Madame d'Aumale was determined, on this
occasion, to keep Octave by her side; she reminded him coaxingly and
without the slightest regard for her male escort, that it was in these
woods that she had seen him for the first time: "You were disguised as
a magician, and never was a first meeting more prophetic," she went
on, "for you have never bored me, and there is no other man of whom I
can say that."

Armance, who was walking with them, could not help feeling that these
memories were very affectionate. Nothing could be so pleasant as to
hear this brilliant Comtesse, so gay as a rule, deigning to speak in
serious tones of the great interests of life and of the courses that
one must follow to find any happiness here below. Octave withdrew
from Madame d'Aumale's group, and, finding himself presently alone
with Armance some little way from the rest of the party, began to
relate to her in the fullest detail the whole of the episode of his
life in which Madame d'Aumale had been involved. "I sought that
brilliant connexion," he told her, "in order not to offend Madame de
Bonnivet, who, but for some such precaution, might easily have
finished by banishing me from her society." So tender a confidence as
this was made without any mention of love, but it was exactly attuned
to Armance's jealousy.

When Armance was able to hope that her voice would not betray the
extreme distress in which this confession had plunged her: "I believe,

my dear cousin," she said to him, "I believe, as I am bound to believe, everything that you tell me; your word to me is as the Gospel. I observe, however, that you have never until now waited, before taking me into your confidence about any of your enterprises, until it was so far advanced." "To that, I have my answer ready. Mademoiselle Méry de Tersan and you take the liberty sometimes of laughing at my success: one evening, for instance, two months ago, you almost accused me of fatuity. I might easily, even then, have confessed to you the decided feeling that I have for Madame d'Aumale; but I should have had to be treated kindly by her in your presence. Before I had succeeded, your malicious wit would not have failed to deride my feeble efforts. To-day, the presence of Mademoiselle de Tersan is the only thing lacking to complete my happiness."

There was in the profound and almost tender accents with which Octave uttered these vain words, such an incapacity to love the somewhat bold charms of the pretty woman of whom he was speaking, and so passionate a devotion to the friend in whom he was confiding that she had not the courage to resist the happiness of seeing herself so dearly loved. She leaned upon Octave's arm, and listened to him as though in an ecstasy. All that her prudence could obtain of her was to refrain from speaking; the sound of her voice would have revealed to her companion the whole extent of the passion by which she was torn. The gentle rustle of the leaves, stirred by the night breeze, seemed to lend a fresh charm to their silence.

Octave gazed into Armance's open eyes which were fastened on his own. Suddenly they became aware of a certain sound which for some minutes had reached their ears without attracting their attention. Madame d'Aumale, surprised at Octave's absence, and feeling the need of his company, was calling to him at the top of her voice. "Some one is calling you," said Armance, and the broken accents in which she uttered these simple words would have enlightened any one but Octave as to the passion that she felt for himself. But he was so astonished by what--was going on in his heart, so disturbed by Armance's shapely arm, barely veiled by a light gauze, which he was pressing to his bosom, that he could pay no attention to anything. He was beside himself, he was tasting the pleasures of the most blissful love, and almost admitted as much to himself. He looked at Armance's hat, which was charming, he gazed into her eyes. Never had Octave found himself in a position so fatal to his vows to refrain from love. He had meant to speak lightly to Armance, as usual, and his light speech had suddenly taken a grave and unexpected turn. He felt himself led away, he was incapable of reason, he was raised to the pinnacle of happiness. It was one of those rapid instants which chance accords now and again, in compensation for so many hardships, to natures that are created to feel with energy. Life becomes pressing in the heart, love makes us forget everything that is not divine like itself, and we live more fully in a few moments than in long periods.

They could still hear from time to time Madame d'Aumale's voice calling: "Octave!" and the sound of that voice succeeded in destroying all poor Armance's prudence. Octave felt that it was time to let go the fair arm that he was pressing gently to his bosom; he must part from Armance; on leaving her he could hardly refrain from taking her hand and pressing it to his lips. Had he permitted himself this token of love, Armance was so disturbed at the moment, that she would have let him see and would perhaps have admitted all that she felt for him. They rejoined the rest of the party. Octave walked a little way ahead. As soon as Madame d'Aumale caught sight of him, she said to him with a trace of vexation, not loud enough for Armance to hear: "I am surprised to see you so soon, how could you leave Armance for me? You are in love with that pretty cousin, do not attempt to deny it; I know." The last words were uttered in a loud voice in contrast to her previous tone.

Octave had not yet recovered from the intoxication that had overpowered him; he still saw Armance's beautiful arm pressed to his bosom. Madame d'Aumale's speech fell on him like a thunderbolt, for it came with the force of truth. He felt the shock of its impact. That frivolous voice seemed to him a pronouncement of fate, falling on him from the clouds. The sound of it seemed to him extraordinary. This startling speech, by revealing to Octave the true state of his heart, dashed him from a pinnacle of bliss into a frightful, hopeless misery.

CHAPTER SEVENTEEN

_What is a man, If his chief good and market of his
time lie but to sleep, and feed? a beast, no more. ...
Rightly to be great
Is not to stir without great argument,
But greatly to find honour in a straw
When honour's at the stake.
   HAMLET, Act IV.

And so he had been so weak as to violate the oaths he had so often
sworn! A single moment had upset the work of his whole life. He had
forfeited all right to his own esteem. Henceforward the world of men
was closed to him; he was not worthy to inhabit it. Nought remained to
him but solitude and a hermit's abode in some wilderness. The
intensity of the grief that he felt and its suddenness might well have
caused some disturbance in the stoutest heart. Fortunately Octave saw
at once that if he did not reply quickly and with the calmest air to
Madame d'Aumale, Armance's reputation might suffer. He spent all his
time with her, and Madame d'Aumale's speech had been seized upon by
two or three people who detested him as well as Armance.
"I, in love!" he said to Madame d'Aumale. "Alas! That is a privilege
which heaven has evidently denied me; I have never felt it so plainly
nor so keenly regretted it. I see every day, though less often than I
could wish, the most attractive woman in Paris; to win her favour is
doubtless the most ambitious project that a man of my age can
entertain. Doubtless she would not have accepted my devotion; still, I
have never felt myself moved to the degree of enthusiasm which would
make me worthy to offer it to her. Never, in her presence, have I lost
the most complete self-possession. After such a display of savagery
and insensibility, I despair of ever going out of my depth with any
woman."
Never had Octave spoken to such effect. This almost diplomatic
explanation was skilfully protracted and received with a corresponding
eagerness. There were present two or three men who were naturally
attractive, and who often imagined that they saw in Octave a fortunate
rival. He was delighted to overhear several sharp comments. He spoke
volubly, continued to alarm their self-esteem, until he felt himself
justified in hoping that no one would pay any further attention to the
all too true observation which Madame d'Aumale had let fall.

She had uttered it with an air of conviction; Octave felt that he must force her to think of herself. Having proved to her that he was incapable of loving her, for the first time in his life he allowed himself to address to Madame d'Aumale allusions that were almost affectionate; she was amazed.

Before the evening ended, Octave was so confident of having banished all suspicions that he began to have time to think of himself. He dreaded the moment when the party would break up, and he would be free to look his misery in the face. He began to count the hours as they sounded from the clock in Andilly; midnight had long since struck, but the night was so fine that they preferred to remain out of doors. One o'clock struck, and Madame d'Aumale dismissed her retinue.

Octave had still a momentary respite. He must go and find his mother's footman and tell him that he was going to sleep in Paris. This duty performed, he returned to the woods, and here words fail me if I am to give any idea of the grief that overpowered the poor wretch. "I am in love," he said to himself in stifled accents. "I, in love! Great God!" and with throbbing heart, parched throat, staring eyes raised to heaven, he stood motionless, as though horror-stricken; presently he began to walk at a headlong pace. Unable to hold himself erect, he let himself fall against the trunk of an old tree that barred his way, and in that moment of repose seemed to see more clearly than ever the whole extent of his misery.

"I had nothing but my own self-esteem," he said to himself; "I have forfeited it." The confession of his love which he made in the plainest terms and without finding any way of denying it was followed by transports of rage and inarticulate cries of fury. Spiritual agony can go no farther.

An idea, the common resource of the wretched who have still some courage, soon occurred to him; but he said to himself: "If I take my life, Armance will be compromised; the whole of society for the next week will be nosing out every trifling detail of what occurred this evening. Armance will be in despair, her despair will be noticed, and each of the gentlemen who was present will be authorised to furnish a different account."

Nothing selfish, no attachment to the vulgar interests of life, could be found in this noble spirit to resist the transports of the frightful grief which was rending it. This absence of all common interest, capable of providing a diversion at such moments, is one of the punishments which heaven seems to take pleasure in inflicting upon lofty spirits.

The hours glided rapidly by without diminishing Octave's despair. Remaining motionless at times for several minutes, he felt that fearful anguish which completes the torment of the greatest criminals: an utter contempt for himself.

He could not weep. The hatred of which he felt himself so deserving prevented him from having any pity for himself, and dried his tears. "Ah!" he cried, in one of those agonising moments, "if I could make an end!" and he gave himself leave to taste the ideal happiness of ceasing to feel. With what pleasure would he have put himself to death, as a punishment of his weakness and to retrieve in a sense his lost honour! "Yes," he told himself, "my heart deserves contempt because it has committed an action which I had forbidden myself on pain of death, and my mind is, if possible, even more contemptible than my heart. I have failed to see what was self-evident: I love Armance, and I have loved her ever since I submitted to listening to Madame de Bonnivet's dissertations upon German philosophy. "I was foolish enough to imagine myself a philosopher. In my idiotic presumption, I regarded myself as infinitely superior to the futile arguments of Madame de Bonnivet, and I failed to see in my heart what the weakest of women would have seen in hers: a strong, obvious passion, which for long has destroyed all the interest that I used to take in the things of life.

"Everything that cannot speak to me of Armance is to me as though it did not exist. I criticised myself incessantly, and failed to see this! Ah, how contemptible I am!"

The voice of duty which was beginning to prevail ordered Octave to shun Mademoiselle de Zohiloff from that instant; but out of her presence he could think of no action that justified the effort of living. Nothing seemed to him worthy to inspire the least interest in him. Everything appeared to him to be equally insipid, the noblest action and the most vulgarly useful occupation alike: to march to the aid of Greece and to seek death by the side of Fabvier, as to make obscure agricultural experiments in some remote Department.

His imagination ran swiftly over the scale of possible actions, to fall back afterwards with an intenser grief into the most profound despair, the most hopeless, the worthiest of his name; ah, how pleasant would death have been at those moments!

Octave uttered aloud things that were foolish and in bad taste, the bad taste and folly of which he observed with interest. "What use in

shutting my eyes to the facts," he exclaimed suddenly, while he was
occupied in enumerating to himself certain agricultural experiments
that might be made among the peasants of Brazil. "What use in being so
cowardly as to shut my eyes to the facts? To complete my misery, I can
say to myself that Armance feels some affection for me, and my duty is
all the stricter in consequence. Why, if Armance were engaged, would
the man to whom she had promised her hand permit her to spend all her
time with me? And her joy, outwardly so calm, but so deep and true,
when I revealed to her last night the secret plan of my conduct with
Madame d'Aumale, to what must it be ascribed? Is it not a proof
positive, as plain as daylight? And I was blind to it! Can I have been
a hypocrite with myself? Can I have been treading the path which the
vilest scoundrels have followed? What! Last night, at ten o'clock, I
failed to perceive a thing which this morning seems as plain as
possible? Ah, how weak and contemptible I am!
"I have all the pride of a child, and never in my whole life have I
risen to perform one manly action; not only have I wrought my own
undoing, I have dragged down into the abyss her who was dearer to me
than any one in the world. Oh, heavens! How could any one, even if he
tried, be viler than I?" This thought left him almost delirious.
Octave felt his brain melt in the fiery heat of his head. At each step
that his mind advanced, he discovered a fresh variety of misery, a
fresh reason for despising himself.
The instinct of self-preservation which exists in every man, even in
the most painful moments, even at the foot of the scaffold, made
Octave try to prevent himself from thinking. He clasped his head in
his hands, making almost a physical effort not to think.
Gradually everything lost its importance for him, except the memory of
Armance whom he must evermore avoid, and never see again upon any
pretext whatsoever. Even filial love, so deeply rooted in his heart,
had vanished from it.
He had now only two ideas, to leave Armance and never allow himself to
set eyes on her again; to support life on these conditions for a year
or two until she were married or society had forgotten him. After
which, as people would then have ceased to think of him, he would be
free to put an end to himself. Such was the last conscious thought of
this spirit exhausted by suffering. Octave leaned against a tree and
fell in a swoon.
When he regained consciousness, he felt an unusual sense of cold. He
opened his eyes. Day was beginning to dawn. He found that he was

receiving the attentions of a peasant who was trying to restore his
consciousness by deluging him with cold water which he fetched in his
hat from a neighbouring spring. Octave was confused for a moment, his
ideas were not clearly defined: he found himself lying upon the bank
of a ditch, in the middle of a clearing, in a wood; he saw great
rounded masses of mist pass rapidly before his eyes. He could not tell
where he was.

Suddenly the thought of all his misfortunes recurred to his mind.
People do not die of grief, or he would have been dead at that moment.
A groan or two escaped him which frightened the peasant. The man's
alarm recalled Octave to a sense of duty. It was essential that this
peasant should not talk. Octave took out his purse to offer him some
money; he said to the man, who seemed to feel some compassion for his
state, that he found himself in the woods at that hour in consequence
of a rash wager, and that it was most important to him that it should
not be known that the cold night air had upset him.

The peasant appeared not to understand. "If the others hear that I
fainted," said Octave, "they will make fun of me." "Ah, I understand,"
said the peasant, "count on me not to breathe a word, it shall never
be said that I made you lose your wager. It is lucky for you all the
same that I happened to pass, for, upon my soul, you looked half
dead." Octave, instead of replying, was gazing at his purse. This was
a further grief, the purse was a present from Armance; he found a
pleasure in feeling with his fingers each of the little steel beads
that were stitched to the dark tissue.

As soon as the peasant had left him, Octave broke off a branch of a
chestnut tree, with which he made a hole in the ground; he allowed
himself to bestow a kiss on the purse, Armance's present, and buried
it beneath the very spot on which he had fainted. "There," he said to
himself, "my first virtuous action. Farewell, farewell for life, dear
Armance! God knows that I loved thee!"

CHAPTER EIGHTEEN

_On her white breast a sparkling
Cross she wore,
Which Jews might kiss, and Infidels adore._
POPE.
[Footnote: Beyle quotes this motto in French, and attributes it to
Schiller.--C. K. S. M.]

A instinctive movement impelled him towards the house. He felt
confusedly that to reason with himself was the greatest misfortune
possible; but he had seen where his duty lay, and hoped to find the
necessary courage to perform such actions as fell to his lot, whatever
they might be. He found an excuse for his return to the house, which
was prompted by his horror of loneliness, in the idea that some
servant might arrive from Paris and report that he had not been seen
in the Rue Saint-Dominique, which might lead to the discovery of his
foolish conduct, and cause his mother some uneasiness.

Octave was still some way from the house: "Ah," he said to himself as
he walked home through the woods, "only yesterday there were boys here
shooting; if a careless boy, firing at a bird from behind a hedge,
were to kill me, I should have no complaint to make. Heavens! How
delightful it would be to receive a bullet in this burning brain! How
I should thank him before I died, if I had time!"

We can see that there was a trace of madness in Octave's attitude this
morning. The romantic hope of being killed by a boy made him slacken
his step, and his mind, with a slight weakness of which he was barely
conscious, refused to consider whether he were justified in so doing.
At length he arrived at the house by the garden gate, and twenty yards
from that gate, at a turn in a path, saw Armance. He stood rooted to
the ground, the blood froze in his veins, he had not expected to come
upon her so soon. As soon as she caught sight of him, Armance hastened
towards him smiling; she had all the airy grace of a bird; never had
she seemed to him so pretty; she was thinking of what he had said to
her overnight about his intimacy with Madame d'Aumale.

"So I am beholding ner for the last time!" Octave said to himself, and
gazed at her hungrily. Armance's wide-brimmed straw hat, her light and
supple form, the long ringlets that dangled over her cheeks in
charming contrast to a gaze so penetrating and at the same time so
gentle, he sought to engrave all these upon his heart. But her

smiling glances, as Armance approached him, soon lost all their joy. She felt there was something sinister in Octave's manner. She noticed that his clothes were wringing wet.

She said to him in a voice tremulons with emotion: "What is the matter, cousin?" As she uttered this simple speech, she could hardly restrain her tears, so strange was the expression she discerned in his gaze.

"Mademoiselle," he replied with a glacial air, "you will permit me to be not unduly sensible of an interest which attaches itself to me so as to deprive me of all freedom. It is true, I have come from Paris; and my clothes are wet: if this explanation does not satisfy your curiosity, I shall go into details...." Here Octave's cruelty came to a standstill in spite of himself.

Armance, whose features had assumed a deathly pallor, seemed to be making vain efforts to withdraw; she was shaking visibly, and seemed to be on the point of falling. He stepped forward to offer her his arm; Armance gazed at him with lifeless eyes, which moreover seemed incapable of receiving any idea.

Octave seized her hand none too gently, placed it beneath his arm and strode towards the house. But he felt that his strength too was failing; on the point of falling himself, he yet had the courage to say to her: "I am going away, I have to start on a long voyage to America; I shall write; I rely upon you to comfort my mother; tell her that I shall certainly return. As for you, Mademoiselle, people have said that I am in love with you; I am far from making any such pretension. Indeed, the old ties of friendship that bound us should have been sufficient, to my mind, to resist the birth of love. We know each other too well to feel for each other that sort of sentiment, which always implies a certain amount of illusion."

At that moment Armance found herself incapable of walking; she raised her drooping eyes and looked at Octave; her pale and trembling lips seemed to be trying to speak. She attempted to lean upon the tub of an orange tree, but had not the strength to support herself; she slipped to the ground by the side of the orange tree, completely unconscious. Without offering her any assistance, Octave stood motionless and gazed at her; she was in a dead faint, her lovely eyes were still half open, the lines of that charming mouth retained an expression of profound grief. All the rare perfection of her delicate body was revealed beneath a simple morning gown. Octave noticed a small cross of diamonds which Armance was wearing that day for the first time.

He was so weak as to take her hand. All his philosophy had evaporated.
He saw that the tub of the orange tree concealed her from the
curiosity of the people in the house; he fell on his knees by her
side: "Pardon me, O my dear angel," he said in a low murmur, covering
her frozen hand with kisses, "never have I loved thee more!"
Armance stirred slightly; Octave rose to his feet, almost with a
convulsive effort: soon Armance was able to walk, and he escorted her
to the house without venturing to look at her. He reproached himself
bitterly for the shameful weakness into which he had let himself be
drawn; had Armance noticed it, all the deliberate cruelty of his words
became useless. She hastily took leave of him on entering the house.
As soon as Madame de Malivert was visible, Octave asked if he might
see her and threw himself into her arms. "Dear Mama, give me leave to
travel, it is the one course open to me if I am to avoid an abhorrent
marriage without failing in the respect I owe to my father." Madame de
Malivert, greatly astonished, tried in vain to extract from her son
any more positive information as to this alleged marriage.
"What!" she said to him, "neither the young lady's name, nor who are
her family, I am to know nothing? But this is madness." Soon Madame
de Malivert no longer dared to employ that word, which, seemed to her
to be too true. All that she could extract from her son, who seemed
determined to start that day, was that he would not go to America. The
goal of his journey was a matter of indifference to Octave, he had
thought only of the pain of departure.
As he was talking to his mother, and trying, in order not to alarm
her, to moderate his feelings, a plausible reason for his action
suddenly occurred to him: "Dear Mama, a man who bears the name of
Malivert and who has the misfortune to have done nothing in the first
twenty years of his life, ought to begin by going on the Crusade like
our ancestors. I beg you to allow me to go to Greece. If you wish, I
shall tell my father that I am going to Naples; from there, quite by
chance, curiosity will lead me on to Greece, and what more natural
than that a gentleman should visit that country sword in hand? By
announcing my itinerary in this way I shall strip it of any air of
pretension...."
This plan caused Madame de Malivert the greatest uneasiness; but there
was a certain nobility in it and it was in accordance with her idea of
duty. After a conversation lasting for two hours, which was a
momentary respite for Octave, he obtained his mother's consent.
Clasped in the arms of that tenderest of friends, he enjoyed for a

brief moment the bliss of being able to weep freely. He agreed to conditions which he would have refused when he entered the room. He promised her that, if she wished it, twelve months from the day of his landing in Greece, he would come and spend a fortnight with her. "But, dear Mama, to spare me the annoyance of seeing my return announced in the newspaper, consent to receive my visit at your place, Malivert, in Dauphiné." Everything was arranged as he wished, and loving tears sealed the terms of this sudden departure.

On leaving his mother's presence, after performing his duty with regard to Armance, Octave found himself sufficiently calm to pay a visit to the Marquis. "Father," he said when he had embraced him, "allow your son to ask you a question: what was the first action of Enguerrand de Malivert, who flourished in 1147, under Louis the Young?"

The Marquis threw open his desk and drew from it a handsome roll of parchment which always lay ready to his hand: it was the pedigree of his family. He saw with intense pleasure that his son's memory had not failed him. "My dear boy," said the old man as he took off his spectacles, "Enguerrand de Malivert started in 1147 on the Crusade with his King." "He was then nineteen, was he not?" Octave went on. "Nineteen exactly," said the Marquis, with growing pleasure in the respect which the young Vicomte shewed for the family tree.

When Octave had given his father's pleasure time to develop and to establish itself firmly in his heart, "Father," he said to him in a firm tone, "_noblesse oblige_. I am now twenty, I have spent time enough with my books. I have come to ask your blessing, and your leave to travel in Italy and Sicily. I shall not conceal from you, but it is to you alone that I am making this admission, that from Sicily I shall be tempted to proceed to Greece; I shall try to take part in a battle and shall return to you, a little more worthy perhaps of the fine name that you have handed down to me."

The Marquis, gallant as he was, had not at all the spirit of his ancestors in the days of Louis the Young; he was a father and a loving father of the nineteenth century. He was left speechless by Octave's sudden resolve; he would gladly have had a son who was less heroic. Nevertheless, this son's austere air, and the firm resolve indicated by his manner made an impression upon him. Strength of character had never been one of his qualities and he dared not refuse a consent that was asked of him with an air of indifference to his possible refusal. "You pierce me to the heart," said the worthy old man as he returned to his desk; and without waiting for his son to ask for it, with a trembling hand he wrote out a draft for a considerable sum upon a notary who held funds in his name. "Take this," he said to Octave, "and pray God it be not the last money that I shall give you!"

The bell rang for luncheon. Fortunately Mesdames d'Aumale and de Bonnivet had gone to Paris; and the members of this sad family were not obliged to conceal their grief with meaningless words.

Octave, somewhat fortified by the consciousness that he had done his duty, found courage to continue. He had thought of starting before luncheon; he felt that it was better to behave as though nothing had happened. The servants might talk. He took his seat at the small luncheon-table, facing Armance.

"It is the last time in my life that I shall see her," he told himself. Armance managed fortunately to burn herself quite seriously while making tea. This accident would have furnished an excuse for her distress, if any one in that small room had been in a fit state to observe it. M. de Malivert's voice was tremulous; for the first time in his life, he could think of nothing pleasant to say. He was wondering whether some pretext compatible with the solemn words "_Noblesse oblige_!" which his son had so aptly quoted, might not furnish him with the means of delaying his son's departure.

CHAPTER NINETEEN

_He unworthy you say?
'Tis impossible.
It would Be more easy to die_.
    DECKAR.
[Footnote: This motto and that prefixed to Chapter XXII are quoted by
Beyle in English, which makes it seem probable that by Deckar he meant
the voluminous writer Thomas Dekker, the "Mr. Dickers" of Henslowe's
Diary, the author of _Satiromastix_ and _The Honest Whore_ and the
Gull's Horn-book and the _Witch of Edmonton_; but this quotation,
which the French editors religiously print in three lines, imagining
it to be a specimen of English poetry, bears the marks of Beyle's
composition.--C. K. S. M.]
Octave thought he observed that Mademoiselle de Zohiloff looked at him
now and again quite calmly. In spite of his peculiar sense of honour,
which formally forbade him to dwell upon relations that no longer
existed, he could not help thinking that this was the first time that
he had seen her since his admission to himself that he loved her; that
morning, in the garden, he had been disturbed by the need for action.
"So this," he told himself, "is the impression a man feels at the
sight of a woman whom he loves. But it is possible that Armance feels
no more than friendship for me. Last night it was only a piece of
presumption on my part that made me think otherwise."
Throughout this distressing meal, not a word was uttered on the
subject that was filling every heart. While Octave was with his
father, Madame de Malivert had sent for Armance to inform her of this
strange plan of foreign travel. The poor girl felt a need of
sincerity; she could not help saying to Madame de Malivert: "Ah, well,
Mama, you see now what foundation there was for your ideas!"
These two charming women were plunged in the bitterest grief. "What is
the reason for this sudden departure?" Madame de Malivert repeated,
"for it cannot be an insane freak; you have cured him of that." It was
agreed that they should not say a word to any one of Octave's travels,
not even to Madame de Bonnivet. It would never do to bind him to his
plan, "and perhaps," said Madame de Malivert, "we may still be allowed
to hope. He will abandon an intention so suddenly conceived. It is the
reaction from some distressing occurrence."
This conversation made Armance's grief more acute, were that possible,

than before; ever loyal to the eternal secrecy which she felt to be due to the sentiment that existed between her cousin and herself, she paid the penalty of her discretion. The words uttered by Madame de Malivert, so prudent a friend and one who loved her so tenderly, since they related to facts of which she was but imperfectly aware, offered no consolation to Armance.

And yet, how sorely she needed the counsels of a woman friend as to the several reasons, any one of which, it seemed to her, might equally well have led to this strange conduct on her cousin's part! But nothing in the world, not even the intense grief that was lacerating her heart, could make her forget the respect that a woman owes to herself. She would have died of shame rather than repeat the words which the man of her choice had addressed to her that morning. "If I made such a disclosure," she told herself, "and Octave were to hear of it, he would cease to respect me."

After luncheon, Octave made hasty preparations to start for Paris. He acted precipitately; he had ceased to account to himself for his movements. He was beginning to feel all the bitterness of his plan of departure and was in dread of the danger of finding himself alone with Armance. If her angelic goodness was not irritated by the frightful harshness of his conduct, if she deigned to speak to him, could he promise himself that he would not be swayed by emotion in bidding farewell to so beautiful, so perfect a cousin?

She would see that he loved her; he must nevertheless leave immediately after, and with the undying remorse of not having done his duty even in that supreme moment. Were not his most sacred duties towards the creature who was dearer to him than any one in the world, and whose tranquillity he had perhaps endangered?

Octave drove out of the courtyard with the feelings of a man going to his death; and in truth he would have been glad to feel no more than the grief of a man who is being led to execution. He had dreaded the loneliness of the journey, he was scarcely conscious of it; he was amazed at this momentary respite which he owed to misery.

He had just received a lesson in modesty too severe for him to attribute this tranquillity to that vain philosophy which had been his pride in the past. In this respect misery had made a new man of him. His strength was exhausted by so many violent efforts and feelings; he was no longer capable of feeling. Scarcely had he come down from Andilly upon the plain before he fell into a lethargic slumber, and he was astonished, on reaching Paris, to find himself being driven by the servant who, when they started, had been at the back of his cabriolet. Armance, hidden in the attic of the house, behind the shutters, had watched every incident of his departure. When Octave's cabriolet had passed out of sight behind the trees, standing motionless at her post, she had said to herself: "All is over, he will not return."

Towards evening, after a long spell of weeping, a question that occurred to her caused her some distraction from her grief. "How in the world could Octave, who is so distinguished for his exquisite manners, and was so attentive, so devoted, perhaps even so tender a friend," she added with a blush, "last night, when we were strolling together, adopt a tone that was so harsh, so insulting, so out of keeping with his character, at an interval of a few hours? Certainly he can have heard nothing about me that could offend him."

Armance sought to recall every detail of her own conduct, with the secret desire to come upon some fault which might justify the odd tone that Octave had adopted towards her. She could find nothing that was reprehensible; she was in despair at not seeing herself in the wrong, when suddenly an old idea came to her mind.

Might not Octave have felt a recurrence of that frenzy which in the past had led him to commit many strange acts of violence? This memory, albeit painful at first, shed a ray of light in her mind. Armance was so wretched that every argument which she was capable of advancing very soon proved to her that this explanation was the most probable. The conviction that Octave had not been unfair, whatever excuse he might have, was to her an extreme consolation.

As for his madness, if he was mad, it only made her love him more passionately. "He will need all my devotion, and never shall that devotion fail him," she added with tears in her eyes, and her heart throbbed with generous courage. "Perhaps at this moment Octave exaggerates the obligation that compels a young gentleman who has done nothing hitherto to go to the aid of Greece. Was not his father anxious, some years ago, to make him assume the Cross of Malta? Several members of his family have been Knights of Malta. Perhaps, since he inherits their fame, he thinks himself obliged to keep the vows which they took to fight the Turks?"

Armance recalled that Octave had said to her on the day on which the news came of the fall of Missolonghi: "I cannot understand the calm tranquillity of my uncle the Commander, he who has taken vows, and, before the Revolution, enjoyed the stipend of a considerable Commandery. And we hope to be respected by the Industrial Party!"

By dint of pondering this comforting way of accounting for her cousin's conduct, Armance said to herself: "Perhaps some personal motive came to reinforce this general obligation by which it is quite possible that Octave's noble soul believes itself to be bound?
"The idea of becoming a priest which he once held, before the success of one section of the clergy, has perhaps been responsible for some recent criticism of him. Perhaps he thinks it more worthy of his name to go to Greece and to shew there that he is no degenerate scion of his ancestors than to seek in Paris some obscure quarrel the grounds of which would always be difficult to explain and might leave a stain?
"He has not told me, because things of that sort are not mentioned to a woman. He is afraid that his habit of confiding in me may lead him to confess it; that accounts for the harshness of his words. He did not wish to be led on to confide in me something that was not proper...."
Thus it was that Armance's imagination strayed among suppositions that were consoling, since they portrayed an Octave innocent and generous. "It is only from excess of virtue," she told herself, with tears in her eyes, "that so generous a being can have the appearance of being in the wrong."

CHAPTER TWENTY

"_A fine woman! a fair woman! a sweet woman!"
"Nay, you must forget that."
"... O, the world hath not a sweeter creature_."
   OTHELLO, Act IV.

While Armance was walking by herself in a part of the woods of Andilly
that was screened from every eye, Octave was in Paris occupied with
preparations for his departure. He was alternating between a sort of
tranquillity, which he was surprised to feel, and moments of the most
poignant despair. Shall we attempt to record the different kinds of
grief that marked every moment of his life? Will not the reader weary
of these melancholy details?

He seemed to hear a continual sound of voices speaking close to his
ear, and this strange and unexpected sensation made it impossible for
him to forget his misery for an instant.

The most insignificant objects reminded him of Armance. So great was
his distraction that he could not see at the head of an advertisement
or on a shop sign an A or a Z without being violently compelled to
think of that Armance de Zohiloff whom he had vowed to himself that he
would forget. This thought fastened upon him like a destroying fire
and with all that attraction of novelty, all the interest he would
have felt in it, if for ages past the idea of his cousin had never
occurred to his mind.

Everything conspired against him; he was helping his servant, the
worthy Voreppe, to pack his pistols; the garrulous talk of the man,
enchanted to be going off alone with his master and to be in charge of
all the arrangements, was some distraction. Suddenly he caught sight
of the words engraved in abbreviated characters on the mounting of one
of the pistols: "Armance tried to fire this weapon, September 3rd,
182--."

He took up a map of Greece; as he unfolded it, there fell out one of
the pins decorated with a tiny red flag with which Armance had marked
the Turkish positions at the time of the siege of Missolonghi.

The map of Greece slipped from his hands. He stood paralysed by
despair. "It is forbidden me, then, to forget!" he cried, raising his
eyes to heaven. In vain did he endeavour to stiffen his resistance.
Everything round about him was stamped with some memory of Armance.
The abbreviated form of that beloved name, followed by some

significant date, was everywhere inscribed.

Octave wandered aimlessly about his room; he kept giving orders which he instantly countermanded. "Ah! I do not know what I want," he told himself in a Paroxysm of grief. "O heavens! What suffering can be greater than this?"

He found no relief in any position. He kept making he strangest movements. If he derived from them a certain surprise and some physical pain, for half an hour, the image of Armance ceased to tonnent him. He tried to inflict on himself a physical pain of some violence whenever his thoughts turned to Armance. Of all the remedies that he could imagine, this was the least ineffectual.

"Ah!" he said to himself at other moments, "I must never see her any more! That is a grief which outweighs all the rest. It is a whetted blade the point of which I must employ to pierce my heart."

He sent his servant to purchase something that would be required on the journey; he needed to be rid of the man's presence; he wished for a few moments to abandon himself to his frightful grief. Constraint seemed to envenom it more than ever.

The servant had not been out of the room for five minutes before it seemed to Octave that he would have found some relief in being able to speak to him; to have to suffer in solitude had become the keenest of torments. "And suicide is impossible!" he cried. He went and stood by the window in the hope of seeing something that would occupy his mind for a moment.

Evening came, intoxication proved powerless to help him. He had hoped to derive a little help from sleep, it only maddened him.

Alarmed by the ideas that came to him, ideas which might make him the talk of the household and indirectly compromise Armance: "it would be better," he told himself, "to give myself leave to make an end of things," and he turned the key in his door.

Night had fallen; standing motionless on the balcony of his window, he gazed at the sky. The slightest sound attracted his attention; but gradually, every sound ceased. This perfect silence, by leaving him entirely to himself, seemed to him to add yet more to the horror of his position. Did his extreme exhaustion procure him an instant of partial repose, the confused hum of human speech which he seemed to hear sounding in his ear made him awake with a start.

Next morning, when his door opened, the mental torment which urged him to take action was so atrocious that he felt a desire to throw his arms round the neck of the barber who was cutting his hair, and to

tell the man how greatly he was to be pitied. It is by a wild shriek
that the wretch who is being tortured by the surgeon's bistouri thinks
to relieve his pain.

In his least unendurable moments, Octave felt the need to make
conversation with his servant. The most childish trivialities seemed
to absorb his whole attention, which he applied to them with a marked
assiduity.

His misery had endowed him with an exaggerated modesty. Did his memory
recall to him any of those little differences of opinion which arise
in society, he was invariably astonished at the positively
discourteous emphasis which he had displayed; it seemed to him that
his adversary had been entirely in the right and himself in the wrong.
The picture of each of the misfortunes which he had encountered in his
life presented itself to him with a Painful intensity; and because he
was not to see Armance again, the memory of that swarm of minor evils
which a glance from her eyes would have made him forget, revived now
with greater bitterness than ever before. He who had so detested
boring visitors began now to long for them. A fool who came to see him
was his benefactor for the space of an hour. He had to write a polite
letter to a distant relative; this ladv was tempted to regard it as a
declaration of love, with such sincerity and profundity did he speak
of himself, so plain was it from his words that the writer stood in
need of pity.

Between these painful alternatives, Octave had reached the evening of
the second day after his parting with Armance; he was coming away from
his saddler's. All his preparations would at last be completed during
the night, and by the following morning he would be free to start.
Ought he to return to Andilly? This was the question that he was
inwardly debating. He perceived with horror that he no longer loved
his mother, for she had no place in the reasons that he advanced for
visiting Andilly again. He dreaded the sight of Mademoiselle de
Zohiloff, all the more because at certain moments he said to himself:
"But is not the whole of my conduct an act of deception?"

He dared not answer: "Yes," whereupon the voice of the tempter said:
"Is it not a sacred duty to visit my poor mother whom I promised that
I would see again?" "No, wretch," cried conscience; "that answer is a
mere subterfuge; you no longer love your mother." At this agonizing
moment his eyes came to rest mechanically upon a playbill, he saw
there the word _Otello_ printed in bold characters. This word recalled
to him the existence of Madame d'Aumale. "Perhaps she has come to

Paris for _Otello_; in that event, it is my duty to speak to her once again. I must make her regard my sudden departure as the idea of a man who is suffering from boredom. I have long kept this plan from my friends; but for many months my departure has been delayed only by pecuniary difficulties of a sort of which a man cannot speak to his wealthy friends."

CHAPTER TWENTY-ONE

Durate, et vosmet rebus servate secundis.
  VlRGIL.
[Footnote: This line, taken from the _Aeneid_ (I, 207), is
inadvertently ascribed by Beyle to Horace.--C. K. S. M.]
Octave entered the Théâtre-Italien; there he-did indeed find Madame
d'Aumale and in her box a certain Marquis de Crêveroche; he was one of
the fops who especially besieged that charming woman; but being less
intelligent or more self-satisfied than the rest, he fancied himself
to enjoy some distinction. As soon as Octave appeared, Madame
d'Aumale had no eyes for any one else, and the Marquis de Crêveroche,
mad with jealousy, left the box without their so much as noticing his
departure.
Octave took his place in the front of the box, and, from force of
habit, for, this evening, he was far from seeking any sort of
affectation, began to talk to Madame d'Aumale in a voice which
sometimes drowned those of the singers. We must confess that he
slightly exceeded the amount of impertinence which is tolerated, and,
if the audience in the stalls of the Théâtre-Italien had been such as
is to be found in the other playhouses, he would have had the
distraction of a public scene.
In the middle of the second act of Otetto, the boy messenger who sells
the _libretti_ of the opera, and proclaims them in nasal accents, came
to him with a note couched as follows:
"I am, Sir, naturally contemptuous of all affectations ; one comes
upon so many in society, that I take notice of them only when they
annoy me. You are annoying me by the racket you are making with the
little d'Aumale. Hold your tongue.
"I have the honour to be, etc.,
"Le marquis de Crêveroche.
"Rue de Verneuil, no. 54."
Octave was profoundly astonished by this note which recalled him to
the sordid concerns of life; he was at first like a man who has been
drawn up for a moment from hell. His first thought was to feign the
joy which soon flooded his heart. He decided that M. de Crêveroche's
opera-glass must be directed at Madame d'Aumale's box, and that this
would give his rival an advantage, if she appeared to be less amused
after the delivery of his note.

This word _rival_ which he employed in his unspoken thoughts made him laugh aloud; there was a strange look in his eyes. "Why, what is the matter?" asked Madame d'Aumale. "I am thinking of my rivals. Can there be anywhere in the world a man who tries to do more to win your favour than I?" This touching reflexion was more precious to the young Comtesse than the most impassioned notes of the sublime Pasta.

Late that night, after escorting home Madame d'Aumale, who wished to sup, Octave, once more master of himself, was calm and cheerful. What a difference from the state in which he had been since the night he spent in the forest!

It was by no means easy for him to find a second. His manner created such a barrier and he had so few friends that he was greatly afraid of being indiscreet should he ask one of his boon companions to accompany him to M. de Crêveroche's. At last he remembered a M. Dolier, an officer on half-pay, whom he saw but seldom, but who was his cousin. At three o'clock in the morning he sent a note to M. Dolier's porter; at half-past five he called in person, and shortly afterwards the two presented themselves at the house of M. de Creveroche, who received them with a politeness that was somewhat mannered but adhered strictly to the forms. "I have been expecting you, gentlemen," he said to them in a careless tone; "I was in hopes that you would be so kind as to do me the honour of taking tea with my friend, M. de Meylan, whom I have the honour to present to you, and myself."

They drank tea. As they rose from table, M. de Crêveroche mentioned the forest of Meudon.

"This gentleman's affected politeness is beginning to make me lose my temper, too," said the officer of the old army as he stepped into Octave's cabriolet. "Let me drive, you must not tire your wrist. How long is it since you were last in a fencing school?" "Three or four years," said Octave, "as far as I can remember." "When did you last fire a pistol?" "Six months ago, perhaps, but I never dreamed of fighting with pistols." "The devil!" said M. Dolier, "six months! This is beginning to be serious. Hold out your arm. You are trembling like a leaf." "That is a weakness I have always had," said Octave.

M. Dolier, greatly annoyed, said not another word. The silent hour that they spent in driving from Paris to Meudon was to Octave the pleasantest moment he had known since his disaster. He had in no way provoked this duel. He meant to defend himself keenly; still, should he be killed, he would be in no way to blame. Situated as he then was, death was for him the greatest good fortune possible.

They arrived at a secluded spot in the forest of Meudon; but M. de Crêveroche, more affected and more of a dandy than ever, offered absurd objections to two or three places. M. Dolier could barely contain himself; Octave had the greatest difficulty in controlling him. "Let me at least talk to the second," said M. Dolier; "I intend to let him know what I think of the pair of them." "Let them wait till to-morrow," Octave checked him in a severe tone; "bear in mind that to-day you have had the privilege of promising to do me a service." M. de Crêveroche's second chose pistols without making any mention of swords. Octave thought this in bad taste and made a sign to M. Dolier who at once agreed. Finally; it was time to fire. M. de Crêveroche, a skilled marksman, scored the first hit; Octave was wounded in the thigh; his blood flowed in streams. "I have the right to fire," he said coolly; and M. de Crêveroche received a graze on the leg. "Bandage my thigh with my handkerchief and your own," Octave said to his servant; "the blood must not flow for some minutes." "Why, what is your idea?" said M. Dolier. "To continue," Octave replied. "I do not feel at all weak, I am just as strong as when we came here; I should carry through any other business, why not make an end of this?" "But it seems to me to be more than finished," said M. Dolier. "And your anger of ten minutes ago, what is become of that?" "The man had no thought of insulting us," replied M. Dolier; "he is merely a fool." The seconds met in conference; both were emphatically opposed to a continuation of the duel. Octave had observed that M. de Crêveroche's second was an inferior creature whom his valour had perhaps thrust into social prominence, but who at heart lived in a state of perpetual adoration of the Marquis; he addressed a few stinging words to the latter. M. de Meylan was reduced to silence by a firm rebuke from his friend, and Octave's second could not in decency open his lips. As he spoke, Octave was perhaps happier than he had ever been in his life. I cannot say what vague and criminal hope he was founding upon a wound that would keep him prisoner for some days in his mother's house, and at no great distance, therefore, from Armance. Finally, M. de Crêveroche, purple with rage, and Octave the happiest of men, succeeded after a quarter of an hour in making their seconds reload their pistols.

M. de Crêveroche, made furious by the fear of not being able to dance for some weeks, owing to the graze on his leg, suggested in vain their firing at one another point blank; the seconds threatened to leave their principals on the ground with their servants and to take the pistols from them if they moved one pace nearer. Luck was once again with M. de Crêveroche; he took a careful aim and wounded Octave severely in the right arm. "Sir," Octave called to him, "you are bound to await my fire, allow me to have my arm bandaged." This operation having been rapidly performed, and Octave's servant, an old soldier, having soaked the handkerchief in brandy which made it cling tightly to the arm; "I feel quite strong," Octave told M. Dolier. He fired, M. de Crêveroche fell, and a minute or two later, died.

Octave, leaning upon his servant's arm, walked back to his cabriolet, into which he climbed without uttering a single word. M. Dolier could not help expressing his pity for the handsome young fellow who lay dying, and whose limbs they could see growing rigid only a few yards away. "It only means one fop the less," said Octave calmly.

Twenty minutes later, although the cabriolet was going at a walking pace, "My arm is hurting me badly," Octave said to M. Dolier, "the handkerchief is too tight," and all of a sudden he fainted. He recovered consciousness only an hour later, in the cottage of a gardener, a kind-hearted fellow whom M. Dolier had taken the precaution of paying liberally as soon as he entered the cottage.

"You know, my dear cousin," Octave said to him, "my mother's delicate health; leave me, go to the Rue Saint-Dominique; if you do not find my mother in Paris, be so extremely kind as to go out to Andilly; tell her, with every possible precaution, that I have had a fall from my horse and have broken a bone in my right arm. Not a word about duels or bullets. I have reason to hope that certain circumstances, about which I shall tell you later, may prevent my mother from being distressed by this slight wound; say nothing about a duel unless to the police, if necessary, and send me a surgeon. If you go on to the mansion house of Andilly, which is five minutes' walk from the village, ask for Mademoiselle Armance de Zohiloff, she will prepare my mother for the story you have to tell her."

The sound of Armance's name revolutionised Octave's situation. So he dared to utter that name, a luxury he had so often forbidden himself! He would not be parted from her for another month, perhaps. It was an exquisite moment.

While the duel was in progress, the thought of Armance had many times occurred to Octave, but he banished it sternly. After mentioning her name, he ventured to think of her for a moment; a little later, he felt very weak. "Ah! If I were to die," he said to himself with joy, and allowed himself to think of Armance as in the days before the fatal discovery of his love for her. Octave observed that the peasants who stood round him appeared greatly alarmed; their evident anxiety diminished his remorse for the liberty he was allowing himself in thinking of his cousin. "If my wounds prove serious," he said to himself, "I shall be allowed to write to her; I have treated her most cruelly."

No sooner had the idea of writing to Armance occurred to him than it took entire possession of Octave's mind. "If I feel better," he said to himself at length, to hush the reproachful voice of conscience, "I shall still be at liberty to burn my letter." Octave was in great pain; his head had begun to ache violently. "I may die at any moment," he told himself cheerfully, making an effort to recall a few scraps of anatomical science. "Ah, surely I am entitled to write!"

In the end he was weak enough to call for pen, paper and ink. There was no difficulty in providing him with a sheet of coarse essay paper and a bad pen; but there was no ink in the house. Dare we confess it? Octave was so childish as to write with his own blood, which continued to ooze from the bandage on his right arm. He wrote with his left hand, and found this less difficult than he had supposed:

"My DEAR COUSIN:

"I have just received two wounds, each of which may confine me to the house for a fortnight. As you are, next to my mother, the person whom I venerate most m the world, I write these lines to give you the above information. Were I in any danger, I should tell you. You have made me accustomed to the proofs of your tender affection; would you be so kind as to pay a call, as though by chance, upon my mother, whom M. Dolier is going to inform of a mere fall from my horse and a fracture of my right arm. Are you aware, my dear Armance, that we have two bones in the part of the arm next to the hand? It is one of those bones that is broken. Of all the injuries that confine one to the house for a month, it is the simplest that I can think of. I do not know whether it will be proper for you to come and see me during my illness; I am afraid not. I intend to do something rash: because of the narrow stair to my room, they will perhaps suggest placing my bed in the sitting-room through which one has to pass to reach my mother's bedroom, and I shall agree. I beg you to burn this letter.... I have just fainted, it is the natural and in no way dangerous effect of a haemorrhage; you see, I am already using scientific terms. You were my last thought as I lost consciousness, my first upon coming to myself. If you think it quite proper, come to Paris before my mother; in the transport of a wounded man, even when it is merely a flesh-wound, there is always something sinister which she must be spared. One of your misfortunes, dear Armance, is that you have lost your parents; if I by any chance (though it is most improbable) die, you will be parted from one who loved you more dearly than a father loves his daughter. I pray to God that He will grant you the happiness that you deserve. That is saying a great, great deal.

"OCTAVE."

"P.S. Forgive my harsh words, which were necessary at the time."

The idea of death having come to Octave, he asked for a second sheet of paper, upon which, in the middle, he wrote:

"I bequeath absolutely everything that I now possess to Mademoiselle Armance de Zohiloff, my cousin, as a trifling token of my gratitude for the care which I am sure that she will take of my mother when I am no longer here.

"Signed at Clamart, the................. 182..

"OCTAVE DE MALJVERT."

And he made two witnesses attest, the nature of his ink leaving him in some doubt as to the validity of the deed.

CHAPTER TWENTY-TWO

To the dull plodding man whose vulgar soul is awake only to the gross and paltry interests of every-day life, the spectacle of a noble being plunged in misfortune by the resistless force of passion, serves only as an object of scorn and ridicule.

   DECKAR.

[Footnote: Compare the motto prefixed to Chapter XIX. This, like the other, is presumably of Beyle's composition.]

As the witnesses completed their attestation, he fainted again; the peasants, greatly concerned, had gone in search of their parish priest.

Finally two surgeons arrived from Paris and pronounced Octave's condition to be serious. These gentlemen realised what a nuisance it would be for them to come every day to Clamart, and decided that the patient should be removed to Paris.

Octave had sent his letter to Armance by an obliging young peasant who engaged a horse from the post and promised to be, within two hours, at the mansion of Andilly. This letter outstripped M. Dolier, who had been kept for some time in Paris looking for surgeons. The young peasant succeeded admirably in having himself admitted to Mademoiselle de Zohiloff's presence without making any stir in the house. She read the letter. She had barely the strength to ask a few questions. Her courage had completely deserted her.

The receipt of these dreadful tidings induced in her that tendency to discouragement which is the sequel to great sacrifices, made at the call of duty but with no immediate effect save tranquillity and inertia. She was trying to accustom herself to the thought that she would never see Octave any more, but the idea of his dying had never once occurred to her. This final blow of fortune took her unprepared. As she listened to the highly alarming details which the young peasant was giving her, she began to sob convulsively, and Mesdames de Bonnivet and de Malivert were in the next room! Armance shuddered at the thought of their hearing her and of having to meet their gaze in the state in which she then was. Such a sight would have been the death of Madame de Malivert, and, in due course, Madame de Bonnivet would have worked it into a tragic and touching anecdote, extremely unpleasant for its heroine.

Mademoiselle de Zohiloff could not, in any case, allow an unhappy

mother to see this letter written in the blood of her son. She settled
upon the plan of going to Paris, accompanied by her maid. The woman
encouraged her to take the young peasant in the carriage with her. I
shall pass over the painful details that were repeated to her during
the drive. They reached the Rue Saint-Dominique.

She shuddered as the carriage came in sight of the house in a bedroom
in which Octave was perhaps drawing his last breath. As it happened,
he had not yet arrived; Armance's last doubt vanished, she was sure
that he was lying dead in the peasant's cottage at Clamart. Her
despair made her incapable of giving the simplest orders; finally she
was able to say that a bed must be made ready in the drawing-room. The
astonished servants did not understand, but obeyed.

Armance had sent out for a hackney carriage, and her one thought was
of how to find an excuse that would allow her to go to Clamart.
Everything, it seemed to her, must give way to the obligation to
succour Octave in his last moments if he still lived. "What is the
world to me, or its vain judgments?" she asked herself. "I considered
it only for his sake; besides, if people are reasonable, they must
approve of my conduct."

Just as she was about to start, she realised, from a clattering sound
at the carriage entrance, that Octave was arriving. The exhaustion
caused by the motion of the journey had made him relapse into a state
of complete unconsciousness. Armance, drawing open a window that
overlooked the court, saw, between the shoulders of the peasants who
were carrying the litter, the pale face of Octave in a dead faint. The
spectacle of that lifeless head, keeping time with the motion of the
litter and swaying from side to side on its pillow, was too painful
for Armance who sank upon the window-sill and lay there motionless.
When the surgeons, after a preliminary dressing of his injuries, came
to report to her upon their patient's condition, as to the one member
of the family that was in the house, they found her speechless,
staring fixedly at them, incapable of replying, and in a state which
they judged to be bordering upon insanity.

She listened incredulously to all that they said to her; she believed
what her own eyes had seen. This most rational young person had lost
all her self-control. Choked by her sobs, she read Octave's letter
over and over again. Carried away by her grief, she dared, in the
presence of a maid, to raise it to her lips. At last, as she re-read
the letter, she saw the injunction to burn it.

Never was any sacrifice more painful; so she must part with all that

remained to her of Octave; still, it was his wish. Notwithstanding her
sobs, Armance set to work to copy the letter; she broke off at every
line, to press it to her lips. Finally she had the courage to burn it
on the marble top of her little table; she gathered up the ashes with
loving care.

Octave's servant, the faithful Voreppe, was sobbing by his master's
bedside; he remembered that he had a second letter written by his
master: it was the will. This document reminded Armance that she was
not the only sufferer. It was incumbent on her to return to Andilly,
to carry news of Octave to his mother. She passed by the bed of the
wounded man, whose extreme pallor and immobility seemed to indicate
the approach of death; he was still breathing, however. To abandon
him in this state to the care of the servants and of a humble surgeon
of the neighbourhood, whom she had called in, was the most painful
sacrifice of all.

On reaching Andilly, Armance found M. Dolier who had not yet seen
Octave's mother; Armance had forgotten that the whole party had gone
off together that morning on an excursion to the Château d'Ecouen.
They had a long time to wait before the ladies returned, and M. Dolier
was able to relate what had occurred that morning: he did not know the
motive of the quarrel with M. de Crèveroche.

Finally they heard the horses enter the courtyard. M. Dolier decided
to withdraw and to appear only in in the event of M. de Malivert's
desiring his presence. Armance, trying to look as little alarmed as
possible, announced to Madame de Malivert that her son had had a fall
from his horse while out riding that morning and had broken a bone in
his right arm. But her sobs, which after the first sentence she was
incapable of controlling, gave the lie to every word of her story.

It would be superfluous to speak of Madame de Mali-vert's despair; the
poor Marquis was dumbfounded.

Madame de Bonnivet, deeply moved herself, and absolutely insisting
upon going with them to Paris, failed completely to restore his
courage. Madame d'Aumale had made off at the first word of Octave's
accident and went at a gallop along the road to the Clichy barrier;
she reached the Rue Saint-Dominique long before the family, learned
the whole truth from Octave's servant and vanished when she heard
Madame de Malivert's carriage stop at the door.

The surgeons had said that in the state of extreme weakness in which
their patient lay every strong emotion must be carefully avoided.
Madame de Mali-vert took her stand behind her son's bed so that she

could watch him without his seeing her.

She sent in haste for her friend, the famous surgeon Duquerrel; on the first day, that able man pronounced favourably upon Octave's injuries; the household began to hope. As for Armance, she had been convinced from the first moment, and was never under the slightest illusion. Octave, not being able to speak to her before so many witnesses, tried once to press her hand.

On the fifth day tetanus appeared. In a moment in which an increase of fever gave him strength, Octave begged M. Duquerrel very seriously to tell him the whole truth.

This surgeon, a man of true courage, who had himself been wounded more than once upon the field of battle by a Cossack lance, answered him: "Sir, I shall not conceal from you that there is danger, but I have seen more than one wounded man in your condition survive tetanus." "In what proportion?" Octave went on.

"Since you are determined to end your life like a man," said M. Duquerrel, "the odds are two to one that in three days you will have ceased to suffer; if you have to make your peace with heaven, now is your time." Octave remained pensive after this announcement but presently his reflexions gave place to a feeling of joy and an emphatic smile. The excellent Duquerrel was alarmed by this joy, which he took to be the first signs of delirium.

CHAPTER TWENTY-THREE

_Tu, sei un niente, o morte! Ma sarebbe mai dopo sceso il primo
gradino délia mia tomba, che mi verrebbe data di veder la vita come
ella è realmente?

GUASCO.

Until that moment Armance had not seen her cousin save in his mother's
presence. That day, after the surgeon had left, Madame de Malivert
thought she could detect in Octave's eyes an unusual access of
strength coupled with a wish to talk to Mademoiselle de Zohiloff. She
asked her young relative to take her place for a moment by her son's
bedside, while she herself went to the next room where she was obliged
to write a letter.

Octave followed his mother with his eyes; as soon as she was out of
sight: "Dear Armance," he said, "I am going to die; there are certain
privileges attached to such a moment, and you will not take offence at
what I am now going to say to you for the first time in my life; I die
as I have lived, loving you with passion; and death is sweet to me,
because it enables me to make you this confession."

Armance was too much overcome to reply; tears welled into her eyes,
and strange to relate, they were tears of happiness. "The most
devoted, the tenderest friendship," she said at length, "binds my
destiny to yours." "I hear you," Octave replied, "I am doubly glad to
die. You bestow on me your friendship, but your heart belongs to
another, to that happy man who has received the promise of your hand."
Octave's accents were too eloquent of misery; Armance had not the
heart to distress him at this supreme moment. "No, my dear cousin,"
she said to him, "I can feel nothing more for you than friendship; but
no one upon earth is dearer to me than you are." "And the marriage of
which you spoke to me?" said Octave. "In all my life I have allowed
myself to tell but that one lie, and I implore you to forgive me. I
saw no other way of opposing a plan suggested to Madame de Malivert by
her extreme interest in my welfare. Never will I be her daughter, but
never shall I love any one more than I love you; it is for you,
cousin, to decide whether you desire my friendship at such a price."
"Were I fated to live, it would make me happy." "I have still a
condition to make," Armance went on. "So that I may venture without
constraint to enjoy the happiness of being perfectly sincere with you,
promise me that, if heaven grants us your life, there shall never be

any question of marriage between us." "What a strange condition!" said Octave. "Are you prepared to swear to me again that you are not in love with any one?" "I swear to you," Armance replied with tears in her eyes, "that never in my life have I loved any one but Octave, and that he is by far the dearest person in the world to me; but I can feel nothing stronger for him than friendship," she added, blushing a deep red at this speech, "and I shall never be able to place any confidence in him unless he gives me his word of honour that, whatever may happen, he will never as long as he lives make any direct or indirect attempt to obtain my hand." "I swear it," said Octave, profoundly astonished... "but will Armance permit me to speak to her of my love?" "It will be the name that you will give to our friendship," said Armance with a bewitching glance. "It is only for the last few days," Octave went on, "that I have known that I love you. This is not to say that, for a very long time back, never have five minutes passed without the memory of Armance arising to determine whether I ought to deem myself fortunate or unfortunate; but I was blind.

"A moment after our conversation in the woods of Andilly, a pleasantry which Madame d'Aumale let fall proved to me that I love you. That night, I tasted the most cruel torments of despair, I felt that I ought to shun you, I made a vow to forget you and to go-away. Next morning, as I returned from the forest, I came upon you in the garden, and spoke to you harshly, in order that your righteous indignation at such atrocious behaviour on my part might arm me with strength to resist the sentiment that was keeping me in France. Had you addressed to me but a single one of those tender words which you have said to me at times in the past, had you looked me in the face, I should never have found the courage that I required to make me go. Do you forgive me?" "You have made me very unhappy, but I had forgiven you before the confession you have just made me."

An hour followed during which Octave for the first time in his life tasted the happiness of speaking of his love to the beloved.

A single utterance had at once altered the whole situation between Octave and Armance; and as for a long time past every moment of the life of each had been occupied in thinking of the other, an astonishment that was full of charm made them forget the approach of death; they could not utter a word to one another without finding fresh reasons for loving one another.

More than once Madame de Malivert had come, on tiptoe, to the door of her own room. She had remained unobserved by two creatures who had forgotten everything, even the cruel death that was waiting to part them. In the end she became afraid that Octave's agitation might increase the peril; she went up to them and said, almost with a laugh: "Are you aware, children, that you have been chattering for more than an hour and a half, it may send up his temperature." "Dear Mama, I can assure you," replied Octave, "that I have not felt so well for four days." He said to Armance: "There is one thing that worries me when my fever is very high. That poor Marquis de Crèveroche had a very fine dog which seemed to be greatly attached to him. I am afraid the poor beast may be neglected now that his master is no more. Could not Voreppe dress up as a gamekeeper and go and buy that fine sporting dog. I should like at least to be certain that it is being well treated. I hope to see it. In any case, I give it to you, my dear cousin."

After this day of agitation, Octave fell into a deep sleep, but on the morrow the tetanus reappeared. M. Duquerrel felt it his duty to speak to the Marquis, and the whole household was plunged in despair. Notwithstanding the stiffness of his nature, Octave was beloved by the servants; they admired his firmness and sense of justice.

As for him, albeit suffering at times the most agonising torments, happier than he had ever yet been in the whole course of his life, the approaching end of that life made him judge of it at last in a rational manner which intensified his love for Armance. It was to her that he was indebted for the few happy moments which he could perceive amid that ocean of bitter sensations and misfortunes. Acting upon her advice, instead of shunning the world, he had acted, and was cured of many false judgments which had increased his misery. Octave was in constant pain, but, greatly to the astonishment of the worthy Duquerrel, he still lived, he had even some strength.

It took him a whole week to renounce the vow never to fall in love which had been the principal motive of his whole life. The approach of death obliged him first of all to forgive himself with sincerity for having violated his oath. "People die as and how they must," he told himself, "but I am dying on the pinnacle of happiness; fortune owed me perhaps this compensation after dooming me continually to such misery. "But I may live," he thought, and was then more embarrassed than before. At length he arrived at the conclusion that, in the unlikely event of his surviving his injuries, the sign of weakness of character would be in his keeping the rash vow made in early youth and not in

breaking it. "For after all the pledge was given solely in the
interests of my own happiness and honour. Why, if I live, may I not
continue to enjoy in Armance's company the delights of that tender
affection which she has sworn for me? Is it within my power not to
feel the passionate love that I have for her?"

Octave was astonished to find himself alive; when at length, after a
week of inward struggle, he had solved all the problems that were
troubling his spirit, and had entirely resigned himself to accepting
the unexpected pleasure which heaven was sending him, in twenty-four
hours there was a complete change in his condition, and the most
pessimistical of the doctors ventured to answer to Madame de Malivert
for her son's life. Shortly afterwards, the fever ceased, and he sank
into a state of extreme weakness, barely able to speak.

On returning to life, Octave was seized with a lasting astonishment;
everything was altered in his eyes. "It seems to me," he said to
Armance, "that before that accident I was mad. Every moment I dreamed
of you, and managed to extract unhappiness from that charming thought.
Instead of making my behaviour conform to the incidents which I
encountered in life, I had made myself an _a priori_ rule anterior to
all experience."

"There is bad philosophy," said Armance with a laugh, "that is why my
aunt was so determined to convert you. You are really mad from excess
of pride, you learned gentlemen; I cannot think why we choose you, for
you are far from merry. For my own part, I despise myself for not
having formed a friendship with some quite inconsequent young man who
talks of nothing but his tilbury."

When he was in full possession of his faculties, Octave continued to
reproach himself with having broken his word; he had fallen slightly
in his own estimation. But the happiness of being able to say
everything to Armance, even the remorse that he felt for loving her
with passion, created, for a person who had never in his life confided
in any one, a state of bliss so far exceeding anything that he had
expected that he never had any serious intention of returning to his
old moods and prejudices.

"When I promised myself that I would never fall in love, I was setting
myself a task beyond human capacity; that is why I have always been
miserable. And that violation of nature lasted for five years! I have
found a heart the like of which I never had the slightest idea could
exist anywhere on earth. Fortune, outwitting my folly, plants
happiness in my way, I take offence at it, I almost fly into a

passion! In what respect am I breaking the law of honour? Who is
there that knew of my vow to reproach me with breaking it? But it is a
contemptible habit, this of forgetting one's promises; is it nothing
to have to blush in one's own sight? But this is a vicious circle;
have I not furnished myself with excellent reasons for breaking that
rash vow made by a boy of sixteen? The existence of a heart like
Armance's excuses everything."

Anyhow, such is the force of habit, Octave found perfect happiness
only with his cousin. He needed her presence.

An uncertainty crept in now and again to trouble Armance's happiness.
She felt that Octave had not taken her completely into his confidence
as to the motives that had led him to avoid her society and to leave
France after the night he had spent in the woods of Andilly. She
considered it beneath her dignity to ask questions, but she did say to
him one day, indeed with a distinct air of severity: "If you wish me
to give way to the inclination which I feel in myself to become your
great friend, you must give me assurances against the fear of being
abandoned at any moment, at the prompting of some odd fancy that may
have entered your head. Promise me that you will never leave the place
in which I am with you, Paris or Andilly or wherever it may be,
without telling me all your reasons." Octave promised.

On the sixtieth day after his injury, he was able to rise, and the
Marquise, who felt keenly the absence of Mademoiselle de Zohiloff,
reclaimed her from Madame de Malivert, who was almost pleased to see
her go.

People are less self-conscious in the intimacy of family life and
during the anxiety of a great sorrow. The dazzling varnish of an
extreme politeness is then less in evidence, and the true qualities of
the heart regain their proper proportions. The want of fortune of this
young relative and her foreign name, which M. de Soubirane was always
careful to mispronounce, had led the Commander, and even M. de
Malivert himself at times, to address her almost as they would have
addressed a paid companion.

Madame de Malivert was trembling lest Octave should perceive this. The
respect which sealed his lips with regard to his father, would have
made him all the more insolent towards M. de Soubirane, and the
Commander's easily irritated vanity would not have failed to take its
revenge in some discreditable anecdote which he would put in
circulation at Mademoiselle de Zohiloff's expense.

These rumours might come to Octave's ears, and, knowing the violence of his nature, Madame de Malivert anticipated the most painful scenes, the most impossible, perhaps, to conceal. Fortunately nothing of all that her somewhat vivid imagination had pictured did occur. Octave had noticed nothing. Armance had turned the tables on M. de Soubirane with a few veiled epigrams on the ferocity of the war which, in recent years, the Knights of Malta had waged upon the Turks, while the Russian officers, with names unknown in history, were taking Ismailoff.

Madame de Malivert, thinking in anticipation of her daughter-in-law's interests, and of the immense disadvantage of entering society without either a fortune or a name, imparted to a few intimate friends confidences intended to discredit beforehand anything that wounded vanity might inspire in M. de Soubirane. These extreme precautions had perhaps not been out of place; but the Commander, who had been gambling on 'Change since his sister's indemnity, and gambling on _certainties_, lost quite a considerable sum, which made him forget all the niceties of his hatred.

After Armance's departure, Octave, who saw her now only in Madame de Bonnivet's presence, began to nourish dark thoughts; his mind dwelt once again upon his old vow. As the wound in his arm gave him constant pain, and even fever at times, the doctors suggested sending him to take the waters at Bareges; but M. Duquerrel, who was intelligent enough not to prescribe the same treatment for all his patients, declared that any air that was at all keen would suffice for his patient's convalescence, and ordered him to spend the autumn on the slopes of Andilly.

This was a spot dear to Octave; by the following day he had removed there. Not that he had any hope of finding Armance there; Madame de Bonnivet had long been speaking of an expedition into the heart of Poitou. She was having restored at great expense the ancient castle in which Admiral de Bonnivet had had the honour, in times past, to entertain François I, and Mademoiselle de Zohiloff was to accompany her.

But the Marquise had had secret information of an approaching list of promotion to the Order of the Holy Spirit. The late King had promised the Blue Riband to M. de Bonnivet. Consequently, the Poitevin architect soon wrote to say that Madame's presence would be superfluous at that moment, since they were short of workmen, and, a few days after Octave's arrival, Madame de Bonnivet came and settled at Andilly.

CHAPTER TWENTY-FOUR

In case the noise made by the servants in moving about their attic quarters should disturb Octave, Madame de Bonnivet transferred them to a peasant's house near at hand. It was in what one might call material considerations of this sort that the Marquise's genius triumphed; she brought an exquisite grace to bear upon what she was doing, and was most skilful in employing her wealth to enhance her reputation for cleverness.

The core of her little world was composed of people who for the last forty years had never done anything that was not strictly conventional, the people who set the fashions and are then surprised at them. These declared that, since Madame de Bonnivet was deliberately sacrificing the prospect of a visit to her estates in the country, and was going instead to spend the autumn at Andilly, in order to keep her dear friend Madame de Malivert company, it was the bounden duty of every one with a heart in his bosom to go out and share her solitude.

So popular was this solitude that the Marquise was obliged to take rooms in the little village down the hill in order to accommodate all the friends who came crowding to see her. She put in wallpapers and beds. Soon half the houses in the village had been decorated under her guidance and were occupied. It became the correct thing to come out from Paris and keep this admirable Marquise, who was looking after that poor Madame de Malivert, company, and Andilly was as thronged with fashion throughout the month of September as any watering-place. This new fashion threatened even to invade the Court. "If we had a score of clever women like Madame de Bonnivet," some one was heard to say, "we might risk going to live at Versailles." And M. de Bonnivet's Blue Riband appeared certain.

Never had Octave been so happy. The Duchesse d'Ancre felt this happiness to be quite natural. "Octave," she said, "may well regard himself as being in a sense the centre of all this movement to Andilly: in the mornings every one sends to inquire after his health; what could be more flattering at his age? That young man is extremely fortunate," the Duchesse went on to say. "He is getting to know the whole of Paris, and it will make him more impertinent than ever." This, however, was not the true reason for Octave's happiness.

He saw that beloved mother, to whom he had given so much cause for anxiety, perfectly happy. She was overjoyed at the brilliant manner in which her son was making his entry into society. Since his triumph, she had begun not to conceal from herself that this kind of distinction was too original and too little copied from recognised types not to need the support of the all-powerful influence of fashion. Failing that reinforcement, it would have passed unnoticed. One of the things that gave Madame de Malivert great pleasure about this time was a conversation that she had with the famous Prince de R------, who came to spend a night at Andilly.

This most outspoken of courtiers, whose word moreover was law in society, appeared to be taking notice of Octave. "Have you observed, as I have, Madame," he said to Madame de Malivert, "that your son never utters a syllable of that _rehearsed wit_ which is the curse of our age? He scorns to appear in a drawing-room armed with his tablets, and his wit varies with the feelings that may be aroused in him. That is why the fools are sometimes so cross with him and withhold their support. When any one succeeds in interesting the Vicomte de Malivert, his wit appears to spring at once from his heart or from his character, and that character seems to me to be one of the strongest. Don't you agree with me, Madame, that character is an organ which has grown obsolete among the men of to-day? Your son seems to me to be destined to play an exceptional part. He is bound to enjoy the very highest reputation among his contemporaries: he is the most solid, and the most obviously solid man that I know. I should like to see him enter the peerage early in life, or to see you get him made Maître des Requêtes." "But," put in Madame de Malivert, almost breathless with the pleasure she felt at the praise of so good a judge, "Octave's success is anything but general."

"All the better," M. de R-------went on with a smile; "it will take the imbeciles of this country three or four years, perhaps, to understand Octave, and you will be able, before any jealousy appears, to push him almost to his proper place; I ask one thing only: restrain your son from appearing in print, he is too well born for that sort of thing."

The Vicomte de Malivert had still a long way to go before he should be worthy of the brilliant horoscope that had been drawn for him; he had still many prejudices to overcome. His distaste for his fellow men was deeply rooted in his heart; were they prosperous, they filled him with revulsion; wretched, the sight of them was more burdensome still. It was only rarely that he had been able to attempt to cure himself of this distaste by a course of good actions. Had he succeeded in this, his unbounded ambition would have thrust him into their midst and into places where fame is purchased with the most costly sacrifices.

At the time of which we are speaking, Octave was far from any thought of a brilliant destiny for himself. Madame de Malivert had had the good sense not to speak to him of the singular future which M. le Prince de R-------predicted for him; it was only with Armance that she ventured to indulge in the blissful discussion of this prophecy.

Armance possessed in a supreme degree the art of banishing from Octave's mind all the annoyances that society caused him. Now that he ventured to confess these to her, she was more and more astonished at the revelation of his singular character. There were still days upon which he would draw the most sinister conclusions from the most casual utterances. There was much talk of him at Andilly. "You are tasting the immediate fruits of celebrity," Armance told him; "people are saying all sorts of foolish things about you. Do you expect a fool, simply because he has the honour to be speaking about you, to find witty things to say?" This was a severe test for a man inclined to take offence.

Armance insisted upon his making her a full and immediate report of all the speeches offensive to himself that he might hear uttered in society. She had no difficulty in proving to him that they had been uttered without any reference to himself, or that they contained only that amount of malice which every one feels towards every one else. Octave's self-esteem had nothing now to keep secret from Armance, and these two young hearts had arrived at that unbounded confidence which is perhaps the most charming thing about love. They could not discuss anything under the sun without secretly comparing the charm of their present taste of mutual confidence with the constraint by which they had been bound a few months earlier when they spoke of the same subjects. And this constraint itself, the memory of which was so strong, and in spite of which they were already, at this period, so happy, was a proof of the old and lasting nature of their friendship.

Next day, on reaching Andilly, Octave was not without some hope that Armance would come there also; he announced that he was ill and kept the house. A few days later, Armance did indeed arrive with Madame de Bonnivet. Octave so arranged that his first outing might take place precisely at seven o'clock in the morning. Armance met him in the garden, where he led her up to an orange tree planted beneath his mother's windows. There, some months earlier, Armance, her heart

wrung by the strange words that he was addressing to her, had fallen
to the ground in a momentary faint. She recognised the spot, smiled,
and leaned against the tub of the orange tree, shutting her eyes. But
for the absence of pallor, she was almost as beautiful as upon the day
when she had fainted for love of him. Octave felt keenly aware of the
change in their relations. He recognised the little diamond cross
which Armance had received from Russia and which was a relic of her
mother. As a rule it was hidden, it was now brought to light by the
movement which Armance made. Octave for a moment lost his senses; he
seized her hand, as upon the day when she had fainted, and his lips
ventured to brush her cheek. Armance drew herself up quickly and
blushed a deep red. She reproached herself bitterly for this
flirtation. "Do you wish to make me angry?" she asked him. "Do you
wish to force me never to leave the house without a maid?"
A breach that lasted for some days was the immediate result of
Octave's indiscretion. But between two people who felt a perfect
attachment to one another, occasions for quarrelling were rare:
whatever Octave might have occasion to do, before considering whether
it would be agreeable to himself, he would seek to discover whether
Armance would be able to see in it a fresh proof of his devotion.
In the evening, when they were at opposite ends of the immense
drawing-room in which Madame de Bonni-vet assembled all the most
remarkable and influential people in the Paris of the day, if Octave
had to answer a question, he would make use of some word which Armance
had just employed, and she could see that the pleasure of repeating
this word made him oblivious of the interest he might otherwise have
felt in what he was saying. Without any deliberate intention, there
grew up thus for the two of them, amid the most delightful and
animated society, not so much a habit of private conversation as a
sort of echo which, without expressing anything distinctly, seemed to
speak of a perfect friendship and an unbounded affection.
May we venture to reproach with a trace of stiffness the extreme
politeness which the present generation thinks itself to have
inherited from that blissful eighteenth century when there was nothing
to hate?
In the midst of this advanced civilisation which for every one of our
actions, however trivial it may be, insists upon furnishing us with a
pattern which we must copy or state our case against it, this
sentiment of sincere and unbounded devotion comes very near to
creating perfect happiness.

Armance never found herself alone with her cousin save in the garden, beneath the windows of the mansion, the ground floor of which was occupied, or in Madame de Malivert's bedroom and in her presence. But this room was very large, and often the frail state of Madame de Malivert's health obliged her to lie down for a little; she would then ask her children (for thus it was that she always spoke of them) to go over to the bay of the window overlooking the garden, so as not to disturb her rest with the sound of their voices. This tranquil, entirely intimate life in the morning hours gave place in the evening to the life of the highest society.

In addition to the people staying in the village, many carriages would come out from Paris, returning after supper. These cloudless days passed rapidly. It never occurred to either of these two young hearts to admit that they were enjoying one of the rarest forms of happiness that is to be met with here below; on the contrary they supposed that they had still many unsatisfied desires. Having no experience of life, they did not see that these fortunate moments could only be of very brief duration. At most, this happiness, wholly sentimental and deriving nothing from vanity or ambition, might have survived in the bosom of some poor family who never saw any strangers. But they were living in society, they were but twenty years old, they were spending all their time together, and, what was the height of imprudence, they let it be guessed that they were happy, and had an air of caring singularly little what society might think. It was bound to have its revenge.

Armance gave no thought to this peril. The only thing that troubled her from time to time was the necessity of renewing her private vow never to accept her cousin's hand, whatever might happen. Madame de Malivert, for her part, was quite calm; she had not the least doubt that her son's present way of life was bringing about an event for which she passionately longed.

Notwithstanding the happy days with which Armance was filling the life of Octave, in her absence there were darker moments in which he pondered the destiny in store for him, and he arrived at the following conclusion: "The most favourable impression of myself reigns in Armance's heart. I might confess to her the strangest things about myself, and, so far from despising me, or taking a horror of me, she would pity me."

Octave told his friend that in his boyhood he had had a passion for stealing. Armance was appalled by the terrible details into which his imagination was pleased to enter as to the lamentable consequences of this strange weakness. This admission overturned her whole existence; she sank into a profound abstraction for which she was scolded; but, before a week had passed since this strange confession, she was pitying Octave and more tender to him, were that possible, than ever before. "He needs my consolation," she told herself, "to make him pardon himself."

Octave, assured by this experience of the unbounded devotion of her whom he loved, and no longer having to conceal his dark thoughts, became far more affable in society; before the confession of his love, induced by the approach of death, he had been an extremely witty and remarkable, rather than an affable young man; he appealed especially to serious people. These thought they could detect in him the _every-day_ side of a man destined to do great things. The idea of duty was too much in evidence in his manner, and went the length at times of giving him an English expression. His misanthropy was interpreted as pride and ill-humour by the older element of society, and shunned the effort to conquer it. Had he been a peer at this date, he would have won a reputation.

It is the want of the hard school of misfortune that often mars the perfection of the young men who were created to be the most charming. In a day, Octave had been formed by the lessons of that terrible master. It may be said that, at the period of which we are speaking, nothing was wanting to the personal beauty of the young Vicomte, or to the brilliant existence which he enjoyed in society. His praises were sung there without ceasing by Mesdames d'Aumale and de Bonnivet and by the older men.

Madame d'Aumale was justified in saying that he was the most attractive man she had ever met, "for he never bores one," was her foolish explanation. "Until I knew him, I had never even dreamed of such a recommendation, and the great thing, after all, is to be amused." "And I," thought Armance as she listened to this artless speech, "I refuse this man who is so welcome everywhere else the permission to clasp my hand; it is a duty," she went on, with a sigh, "and never shall I fail to observe it." There were evenings on which Octave indulged in the supreme happiness of not talking, and of watching the spectacle of Armance, as presented before his eyes. These moments did not pass unobserved, either by Madame d'Aumale, vexed that any one should neglect to provide her with amusement, or by Armance, delighted to see the man she adored occupied exclusively with herself.

The list of promotions in the Order of the Holy Spirit appeared to
have been delayed; it was a question of Madame de Bonnivet's departure
for the old castle situated in the heart of Poitou, which had given
its name to the family. A new personage was to join the expedition,
namely, M. le Chevalier de Bonnivet, the youngest of the sons that the
Marquis had had by a former marriage.

CHAPTER TWENTY-FIVE

Totus mundus stult.

HUNGARIAE R-----

About the time of Octave's wound, a fresh person had arrived from
Saint-Acheul to join the Marquise's party. This was the Chevalier de
Bonnivet, her husband's third son.

Had the old order been still in existence, he would have been destined
for Episcopal rank, and, albeit many things have now changed, a sort
of family tradition had persuaded everybody, himself included, that he
ought to belong to the Church.

This young man, who was barely twenty, was supposed to be very clever;
his chief characteristic was a wisdom beyond his years. He was a
little creature, very pale; he had a plump face, and, taking him all
round, a somewhat priestly air.

One evening the _Etoile_ was brought in. The single paper band that is
used to wrap this newspaper happened to be displaced; it was evident
that the porter had read it. "And this paper, too!" was the Chevalier
de Bonnivet's impulsive exclamation, "simply to save the cost of a
second band of grey paper, folded across the other, it is not afraid
of running the risk of letting the lower orders read it, as though the
lower orders were intended to read! As though the lower orders were
capable of distinguishing good from evil! What are we to expect of the
Jacobin papers when we see the Monarchist sheets behave like this?"
This burst of spontaneous eloquence greatly enhanced the Chevalier's
reputation. It at once brought over to his side the elderly people and
every one who in Andilly society had more pretensions than wit. The
taciturn Baron de Bisset, whom the reader may perhaps remember, rose
gravely and crossed the room to embrace the Chevalier without uttering
a word. This action cast an air of solemnity over the room for some
minutes and amused Madame d'Aumale. She called the Chevalier to her
side, tried to make him talk, and took him to some extent under her
wing.

All the young women followed in her wake. They made the Chevalier a
sort of rival to Octave, who had already been wounded and was confined
to the house, in Paris.

But presently they began to find that the Chevalier de Bonnivet, young
as he was, gave them a sense of revulsion. He was felt to be
singularly wanting in sympathy with all the things in which people are

interested. The young man had a future of his own. There might be
detected in him an element of deeply rooted treachery towards every
one in the world.

On the day following that on which he had shone at the expense of the
Etoile, the Chevalier de Bonnivet, who saw Madame d'Aumale from an
early hour, opened the ball with her on the lines of Tartufe when he
offers a handkerchief to Dorine so that she may cover "things which
ought not to be seen." He read her a serious lecture upon some
frivolous remark which she had just made about a procession.

The young Comtesse retorted sharply, brought him repeatedly back to
the charge, and was in ecstasies at his absurdity. "He is just like my
husband," she thought. "What a pity poor Octave is not here, how we
should laugh!"

The Chevalier de Bonnivet was shocked more than by anvthing else by
the sort of renown that clung to the Vicomte de Malivert, whose name
he heard upon every tongue. Octave came to Andilly and reappeared in
society. The Chevalier supposed him to be in love with Madame
d'Aumalc, and, with this idea in his head, formed the plan of
developing a passion for the pretty Comtesse, with whom he was most
affable.

The Chevalier's conversation was a perpetual and very clever string of
allusions to the masterpieces of the great writers and poets of French
and Latin literature. Madame d'Aumalc, whose knowledge was scanty,
made him explain the allusions to her, and nothing amused her more.
The Chevalier's really astounding memory did him good service; he
repeated without hesitation the lines of Racine or the passages from
Bossuet to which he had referred, and indicated clearly and elegantly
the bearing of the allusion he had intended to make upon the subject
of their conversation. All this had the charm of novelty in the eyes
of Madame d'Aumale.

One day the Chevalier said: "A single short article in _La Pandore_ is
enough to spoil all the pleasure that we derive from power." This was
considered very deep.

Madame d'Aumale greatly admired the Chevalier; but after a very few
weeks had passed he had begun to alarm her. "You have the effect upon
me," she told him, "of a venomous animal encountered in some solitary
spot in the heart of the forest. The cleverer you are, the more
capable you become of doing me harm."

Another day she said to him that she would wager that he had of his
own initiative discovered the great principle: that speech was given

to man to enable him to conceal his thoughts.

The Chevalier had been highly successful with the rest of society. For instance, although separated from his father for the last eight years, which he had spent at Saint-Acheul, Brig, and elsewhere, often without the Marquis's even knowing where he was, once he had returned and was living with him, in less than two months he succeeded in acquiring a complete domination over the mind of the old man, one of the shrewdest courtiers of the time.

M. de Bonnivet had always been afraid of seeing the French Restoration end like the English; but for the last year or so this fear had made a regular miser of him. Society was therefore greatly astonished to see him give thirty thousand francs to his son the Chevalier, as a contribution to the foundation of certain houses of Jesuits.

Every evening, at Andilly, the Chevalier used to recite prayers, together with the forty or fifty servants in attendance upon the people who were staying in the mansion or in the peasants' houses that had been secured for the Marquise's friends. These prayers were followed by a short exhortation, improvised and very well expressed. The elderly women began to make their way to the orangery, where these evening exercises were held. The Chevalier had it decorated with charming flowers, constantly renewed, for which he sent to Paris. Soon this pious and severe exhortation began to arouse a general interest; it was in marked contrast to the frivolous manner in which the rest of the evening was spent.

Commander de Soubirane declared himself one of the warmest supporters of this method of leading back to good principles all the subordinates who of necessity surround important persons and who, he would add, shewed such cruelty the moment the reign of terror began. This was a favourite expression with the Commander, who went about everywhere announcing that within ten years, unless we re-established the Knights of Malta and the Jesuits, we should have a second Robespierre.

Madame de Bonnivet had not failed to send to her son-in-law's pious exercises those of her own people whom she could trust. She was greatly astonished to learn that he made doles of money to the servants who came to confide to him in private that they were in want. The list of promotions in the Order of the Holy Spirit being apparently delayed, Madame de Bonnivet announced that her architect had written to her from Poitou that he had managed to collect a sufficient number of workmen. She made her preparations for the journey, as did Armance. She was none too well pleased when the

Chevalier de Bonnivet announced his intention of accompanying her to Bonnivet, in order, he said, to see once more the old castle, the cradle of his race.

The Chevalier saw quite well that his presence annoyed his mother-in-law; all the more reason for him to accompany her on this expedition. He hoped to impress Armance by recalling the glories of his ancestors; for he had noticed that Armance was friends with the Vicomte de Malivert, and intended to take her from him. These projects, long under consideration, became apparent only at the moment of their execution.

No less successful with the young people than with the more serious element of society, before leaving An-dilly, the Chevalier de Bonnivet had managed artfully to fill Octave with jealousy. After the departure of Armance, Octave even began to think that this Chevalier de Bonnivet, who boasted an esteem and a respect for her that were unbounded, might well be that mysterious suitor whom an old friend of her mother had found for her.

On taking leave of one another, Armance and her cousin were alike tormented by dark suspicions. Armance felt that she was leaving Octave with Madame d'Aumale; but she did not think that she could allow herself to write to him.

During this cruel separation, Octave could do nothing but address to Madame Bonnivet two or three letters, quite charming but couched in a singular tone. Had any one who was a stranger to their society seen these letters, he would have thought that Octave was madly in love with Madame de Bonnivet and dared not confess his love to her.

In the course of this month of absence, Mademoiselle de Zohiloff, whose good sense was no longer troubled by the bliss of being under the same roof as her friend and of seeing him thrice daily, made some severe reflexions. Albeit her behaviour had been perfectly proper, she could not blind herself to the fact that it must be easy to read the exnression in her eyes when she looked at her cousin.

The promiscuity of travel was the cause of her overhearing a conversation among Madame de Bonnivet's maids which drew many tears from her eyes. These women, like every one who is connected with persons of importance, seeing nothing anywhere but pecuniary interests, set down to this motive the appearance of passion which Armance was assuming, they said, in order to become Vicomtesse de Malivert; no small matter to a penniless girl of such obscure birth.

The idea of her being slandered to such a degree had never occurred to

Armance. "I am a ruined girl," she said to herself; "my feeling for
Octave has passed beyond suspicion, and even that is not the worst of
my supposed offences. I live under the same roof as he, and it is not
possible for him to marry me...." From that instant, the thought of
the slanders that were being uttered against her, resisting every
argument that Armance could advance, poisoned her life.
There were moments in which she fancied that she had forgotten even
her love for Octave. "Marriage is not intended for a girl in my
position. I shall not marry him;" she thought; "and I shall have to
live far more apart from him. If he forgets me, as is highly probable,
I shall go and end my days in a convent; that will be a very proper
asylum, and greatly to be desired, for the rest of my existence. I
shall think of him, I shall hear of his triumphs. People in society
will be able to recall many examples of lives similar to that which I
shall be leading."
These precautions were sound; but the thought, terrible for a girl,
that she might, with some appearance of justice, be exposed to the
slander of a whole household, and that the household in which Octave
was living, cast a shadow over Armance's life which nothing could
dissipate. Did she endeavour to escape from the memory of her
misdeeds, for this was the name she gave to the sort of life she had
led at Andilly, she would begin to think of Madame d'Aumale, whose
attractions she would unconsciously exaggerate. Chevalier de
Bonnivet's company made her regard as even more irremediable than they
actually are all the harm that society can do us when we have offended
it. Towards the end of her stay at the old Château de Bonnivet,
Armance spent every night in weeping. Her aunt noticed this
melancholy, and did not conceal from the girl how angry it made her.
It was during her stay in Poitou that Armance learned of an event
which affected her but little. She had three uncles in the Russian
service; these young men perished by suicide during the troubles in
that country. Their death was kept secret; but finally, after many
months, some letters which the police had not succeeded in
intercepting were delivered to Mademoiselle de Zohiloff. She had
succeeded to a comfortable fortune, which would make her a suitable
match for Octave.
This event was not calculated to appease the anger of Madame de
Bonnivet, to whom Armance was necessary. The poor girl had to listen
to some very sharp comments on the preference that she shewed for
Madame de Malivert's drawing-room. Great ladies are no more spiteful

than the average rich woman; but one acquires in their society a
greater susceptibilty, and feels more profoundly and, if I may venture
to use the expression, more irremediably, their unpleasant remarks.
Armance supposed that nothing was wanting to complete her misery, when
the Chevalier de Bonnivet informed her, one morning, with the
indifferent air which people assume in repeating a piece of news which
is already stale, that Octave was again far from well, and that the
wound in his arm had opened and was causing anxiety. Since Armance had
left him, Octave, who had become hard to please, was often bored with
his mother's drawing-room. He was guilty of acts of imprudence when
shooting, which had serious consequences. He had had the idea of
using a little gun, very light, which he fired with his left hand; his
success with this weapon encouraged him.
One day, as he was going after a winged partridge, he jumped a ditch
and hit his arm against a tree, which brought back his fever. During
this fever and the state of weakness that followed it, the artificial
happiness, so to speak, which he had enjoyed in the company of
Armance, seemed to have become as unsubstantial as a dream.
Mademoiselle de Zohiloff returned at length to Paris, and the
following day, at Andilly, the lovers met once more; but they were
very sad, and this sorrow was of the worst possible kind: it sprang
from a mutual doubt. Armance did not know what tone to adopt with her
cousin; and they barely spoke to one another the first day.
While Madame de Bonnivet was indulging in the pleasure of building
gothic towers in Poitou and imagining that she was reconstructing the
twelfth century, Madame d'Aumale had taken decisive action to ensure
the great triumph which came at last to crown the long-nourished
ambition of M. de Bonnivet. She was the heroine of Andilly. In order
not to have to part with so valuable a friend, during her own absence,
Madame del Bonnivet had made the Comtesse d'Aumale agree to occupy a
little apartment in the highest part of the mansion, close to Octave's
room. And Madame d'Aumale seemed to every one to be perfectly well
aware that it was in a sense for her sake that Octave had received the
wound which was causing his fever. It was in extremely bad taste to
remind people of the affair, which had cost the Marquis de Crêveroche
his life; Madame d'Aumale could not, however, refrain from making
frequent allusions to it: the fact is that the way of the world is to
natural delicacy pretty much what science is to the mind. Her
character, entirely on the surface and not at all romantic, was
impressed first and foremost by realities. Armance had not been more

than a few hours at Andilly before this constant recurrence to the same topics, by a mind that as a rule was so frivolous, struck her forcibly.

Armance arrived there very sad and greatly discouraged; she felt for the second time in her life the assault of a sentiment that is terrifying, especially when it coincides in a single heart with an exquisite sense of the proprieties. Armance imagined that she had serious fault to find with herself in this respect. "I must keep a strict watch over myself," she said to herself as she turned away her gaze, which was resting on Octave, to examine the brilliant Comtesse d'Aumale. And each separate charm of the Comtesse was for Armance the occasion of an excessive act of humility. "How could Octave fail to give her the preference?" she said to herself; "I myself feel that she is adorable."

Such painful sentiments, combined with the remorse which Armance was feeling, wrongly no doubt, but none the less painfully for that, made her far from affable to Octave. On the morning after her arrival, she did not come down betimes to the garden; this had been her habit in the past, and she knew very well that Octave was waiting for her there.

In the course of the day, Octave spoke to her two or three times. An extreme shyness which seized her, with the thought that everybody was watching them, paralysed her, and she barely answered him.

That day, at dinner, mention was made of the fortune which chance had just brought to Armance; and she observed that the news seemed to give little pleasure to Octave, who did not say a single word to her about it. The word that was not uttered, had her cousin addressed it to her, would not have given birth in her heart to a pleasure equivalent to one hundredth part of the grief which his silence caused her.

Octave was not listening; he was thinking of the singular manner that Armance had adopted towards him since her return. "No doubt she no longer cares for me," he was saying to himself, "or she has made some definite engagement with the Chevalier de Bonnivet." Octave's indifference to the news of Armance's fortune opened for the poor girl a fountain of sorrows both new and deep. For the first time, she thought long and earnestly of this inheritance which had come to her from the North, and which, had Octave loved her, would have made her a more or less suitable match for him.

Octave, to obtain an excuse for writing her a page, had sent to her, in Poitou, a short poem about Greece which had just been published by

Lady Nelcombe, a young Englishwoman who was a friend of Madame de
Bonnivet. In the whole of France there were but two copies of this
poem, which was greatly discussed. Had the copy which had made the
journey to Poitou appeared in the drawing-room, a score of indiscreet
attempts would have been made to intercept it; Octave begged his
cousin to have it sent to his room. Armance, greatly intimidated,
could not summon up courage to entrust such a mission to her maid. She
went up to the second floor of the mansion and placed the little
English poem on the handle of Octave's door, so that he could not
enter his room without noticing it.

Octave was greatly troubled; he saw that Armance was definitely
reluctant to speak to him. Feeling himself by no means in the humour
to speak to her, he left the drawing-room before ten o'clock. He was
agitated by a thousand sinister thoughts. Madame d'Aumale was soon
bored with the drawing-room: they were talking politics, and in a
depressing tone; she pleaded a headache, and by half-past ten had
retired to her own apartment. Probably Octave and Madame d'Aumale were
taking a stroll together; this idea, which occurred to every one, made
Armance turn pale. Whereupon she reproached herself with her very
grief as an impropriety which made her less worthy of her cousin's
esteem.

Next morning, at an early hour, Armance was with Madame de Malivert,
who needed a particular hat. Her maid had gone to the village; Armance
hurried to the room in which the hat was; she was obliged to pass by
the door of Octave's room. She stood as though thunderstruck on
catching sight of the little English poem balanced upon the handle of
the door, exactly as she had left it overnight. It was evident that
Octave had not gone to his own room.

This was the absolute truth. He had gone out shooting, notwithstanding
the recent accident to his arm; and, so as to be able to rise betimes
and unobserved, had spent the night in the game-keeper's cottage. He
intended to return to the house at eleven, when the bell rang for
luncheon, and thus to escape the reproaches which would have been
heaped on him for his imprudence.

On returning to Madame de Malivert's room, Armance found herself
obliged to say that she was unwell. From that moment she was a
different person. "I am bearing a fit punishment," she told herself,
"for the false position in which I have placed myself, and which is so
improper in a young person. I have come to the stage of sufferings
which I cannot admit even to myself."

When she saw Octave again, Armance had not the courage to put to him any question as to the accident which had prevented him from seeing the little English poem; she would have felt that she was wanting in everything that she owed to herself. This third day was even more sombre than those that had gone before.

CHAPTER TWENTY-SIX

Octave, aghast at the alteration which he noticed in Armance's manner,
thought that, even as a mere friend, he might hope that she would
confide in him the cause of her anxiety; for that she was unhappy he
could have no doubt. It was equally clear to him that the Chevalier de
Bonnivet was seeking to rob them of every opportunity of exchanging a
word in private which chance might offer them on a walk or in the
drawing-room.

The hints which Octave threw out now and again met with no response.
If she were to confess her grief and abandon the systematic restraint
to which she had subjected herself, Armance would first have had to be
profoundly moved; Octave was too young and too wretched himself to
make this discovery or to profit by it.

Commander de Soubirane had come to dine at Andilly; there was a storm
that evening, it rained in torrents. The Commander was invited to
stay the night, and was given a room next to the one into which Octave
had recently moved, on the second floor. That evening Octave had set
himself to revive a little of Armance's gaiety; he wanted to see her
smile; he would have seen in that smile a presentment of their old
friendship. His gaiety failed completely, and greatly annoyed
Armance. As she did not answer him, he was obliged to address his fine
speeches to Madame d'Aumale, who was one of the circle and laughed
constantly, while Armance preserved a grim silence.

Octave ventured to put a question to her which seemed to require a
fairly long answer: he was answered in two words, most drily. In
desperation at this proof of his disgrace, he left the room
immediately. As he took the air in the garden, he met the game-keeper,
and told him that he would be going out shooting early next morning.
Madame d'Aumale, seeing only serious people in the drawing-room whose
conversation she found burdensome, decided to retire and did so. This
second assignation seemed plain as daylight to the wretched Armance.
Furious above all at the duplicity of Octave, who, only that evening,
as they passed from one room to the next, had murmured a few very
tender words in her ear, she went up to her own room to fetch a volume
which she intended to balance, like the little English poem, upon the
handle of Octave's door. As she advanced along the corridor which led
to her cousin's room, she heard a sound from within; his door stood
ajar, and he was priming his gun. There was a small closet which

served as a second entrance to the room that had, been prepared for the Commander, and the door of this closet opened upon the corridor. As ill luck would have it, this door was open. Octave came to the door of his room as Armance approached, and made a movement as though of emerging into the passage. It would have been frightful for Armance to be discovered by Octave at that moment. She had barely time to fling herself behind the open door that offered a way of escape. "As soon as Octave has gone," she said to herself, "I shall arrange the book." She was so troubled by the thought of the liberty she was allowing herself to take, which was a great sin, that she was barely capable of reasoning connectedly.

Octave did indeed come out of his room; he passed by the open door of the little closet in which Armance was hiding; but he went no farther than the end of the corridor. He leaned out of one of the windows and whistled twice, as though to give a signal. As the game-keeper, who was drinking in the servants' hall, did not reply, Octave remained at the window. The silence that reigned in this part of the house, the guests being assembled in the drawing-room on the ground floor and the servants in the basement, was so profound that Armance, whose heart was beating violently, dared not move a muscle. Besides, poor Armance could not blind herself to the fact that Octave had given a signal; and, however unsuited it might be to a lady, it seemed to her that it was one that Madame d'Aumale might very well have arranged. The window from which Octave was leaning was at the head of the little stair leading down to the first floor, it was impossible for her to pass him. Octave whistled a third time as the clock finished striking eleven; the game-keeper, who was with the others in the servants' hall, did not answer. About half-past eleven, Octave returned to his room.

Armance, who had never in her life been engaged in any enterprise for which she need blush, was so much upset that she found herself unable to walk. It was evident that Octave was giving a signal; either some one would answer or presently he would come out of his room again. The third quarter sounded from the stable clock, then midnight. The lateness of the hour increased Armance's misgivings; she decided to leave the closet which had given her shelter, and as the last of the twelve strokes sounded she stepped forth. She was so much upset that she, whose step was usually light, made quite a loud noise.

As she moved along the corridor, she caught sight of a figure in the darkness, by the window at the head of the stair, outlined against the sky, and at once recognised M. de Soubirane. He was waiting for his servant to bring him a candle, and, as Armance stood motionless gazing at the face of the Commander whom she had just recognised, the light of the candle, which was now being carried upstairs, appeared upon the ceiling of the corridor.

Had she kept her head Armance might have attempted to hide behind a big cupboard which stood in the corner of the corridor, near the stair, and might thus have been saved. Rooted to the ground with terror, she lost a moment or two, and, as the servant reached the head of the stair, the light of the candle shone full upon her, and the Commander recognised her. A hideous smile appeared on his lips. His suspicions of the understanding between Armance and his nephew were confirmed, while at the same time he had found a way to ruin them for ever. "Saint-Pierre," he said to his servant, "is not that Mademoiselle Armance de Zohiloff standing there?" "Yes, Sir," said the servant, greatly confused. "Octave is better, I hope, Mademoiselle?" said the Commander in a coarse, bantering tone, and walked past her.

CHAPTER TWENTY-SEVEN

Armance, in despair, saw herself at once disgraced for ever and
betrayed by her lover. She sat down for a moment on the landing of the
stair. She decided to go and knock at the door of Madame de Malivert's
maid. The girl was asleep and did not answer. Madame de Malivert, with
a vague fear that her son might be ill, took her nightlight and came
to the door of her own room; she was alarmed by the expression on
Armance's face. "What has happened to Octave?" cried Madame de
Malivert. "Nothing, Madame, nothing at all to Octave, it is only I who
am in distress and miserable at having disturbed your sleep. My idea
was to speak to Madame Dérien and to ask for you only if I was told
that you were still awake." "My child, you increase my alarm with all
these _Madames_. Something strange has happened. Is Octave ill?" "No,
Mama," said Armance and burst into tears, "it is only that I am a
ruined girl."

Madame de Malivert took her into her bedroom, and there Armance told
her what had just happened to her, concealing nothing and passing
nothing over in silence, not even her own jealousy. Her heart, crushed
by all her miseries, had not the strength to keep anything back.
Madame de Malivert was appalled. Suddenly she exclaimed: "There is no
time to be lost, give me my pelisse, my poor child, my dear child,"
and she kissed her again and again with all the passion of a mother.
"Light my candle, and do you stay here." Madame de Malivert ran to her
son's room; fortunately the door was not locked; she entered quietly,
awoke Octave and told him what had occurred. "My brother may ruin us,"
said Madame de Malivert, "and, to judge by appearances, he will not
miss the opportunity. Rise, go to his room, tell him that I have had a
sort of seizure in your room. Can you think of anything better?" "Yes,
Mama, to marry Armance to-morrow, if that angel will still have me."
This unexpected speech was a fulfilment of Madame de Malivert's
dearest wish; she embraced her son, but added, on second thoughts:
"Your uncle does not like Armance, he may talk; he will promise to
keep silence, but he has his servant who will talk by his order, and
whom he will then dismiss for having talked. I stick to my idea of a
seizure. This make-believe will keep us painfully busy for three days,
but your wife's honour is more precious than anything else. Remember
to appear greatly alarmed. As soon as you have told the Commander, go
down to my room, tell Armance of our plan. When the Commander passed

her on the stair, I was in your room, and she was going to fetch Madame Dérien." Octave hastened to tell his uncle, whom he found wide awake. The Commander looked at him with a derisive expression which turned all his emotion to anger. Octave left M. de Soubirane to fly to his mother's room: "Is it possible," he said to Armance, "that you have not been in love with the Chevalier de Bonnivet, and that he is not the mysterious husband of whom you spoke to me once, long ago?" "I have a horror of the Chevalier. But you, Octave, are not you in love with Madame d'Aumale?" "Never as long as I live will I see her again or give her another thought," said Octave. "Dear Armance, deign to say that you accept me as a husband. Heaven is punishing me for having kept you in the dark as to my shooting expeditions, I was whistling for the keeper, who did not answer." Octave's protestations had all the warmth but not all the delicacy of true passion; Armance thought she could make out that he was performing a duty while his thoughts were elsewhere. "You are not in love with me just now," she said to him. "I love you with all my heart and soul, but I am mad with rage at that ignoble Commander, vile man, upon whose silence we cannot count." Octave renewed his solicitations. "Are you sure that it is love that is speaking," Armance said to him, "perhaps it is only generosity, and you are in love with Madame d'Aumale. You used to have a horror of marriage, this sudden conversion seems to me suspicious." "In heaven's name, dear Armance, do not let us waste any more time; all the rest of my life shall answer to you for my love." He was so far convinced of the truth of what he was saying that he ended by convincing her also. He hastened upstairs and found the Commander with his mother, whom her joy at the prospect of Octave's marriage had given the courage to play her part admirably. Nevertheless, the Commander did not seem to be at all convinced of his sister's seizure. He ventured upon a pleasantry with regard to Armance's nocturnal roamings. "Sir, I have still one sound arm," cried Octave, springing to his feet and throwing himself upon him; "if you say one word more, I shall fling you out of that window." Octave's restrained fury made the Commander blench, he remembered in time his nephew's mad outbursts and saw that he was worked up to the pitch of committing a crime.

Armance appeared at that moment, but Octave could think of nothing to say to her. He could not even look lovingly at her, this calm after the storm left him powerless. The Commander, to make the best of a bad business, having tried to say something light and pleasant, Octave was afraid of his wounding Mademoiselle de Zohiloff's feelings. "Sir," he

said to him, gripping his arm tightly. "I must ask you to withdraw at
once to your own room." As the Commander hesitated, Octave seized him
by the arm, carried him off to his room, flung him inside, locked the
door, and put the key in his pocket.

When he rejoined the ladies he was furious. "If I do not kill that
base and mercenary creature," he cried, as though talking to himself,
"he will dare to speak evil of my wife. A curse upon him!"

"As far as I am concerned, I like M. de Soubirane," said Armance in
her alarm, seeing the distress that Octave was causing his mother. "I
like M. de Soubirane, and if you go on being furious I may think that
you are cross because of a certain rather sudden engagement which we
have just announced to him."

"You do not believe it," Octave interrupted her, "I am sure of that.
But you are right, as you always are. When all is said and done, I
ought to be thankful to that base creature;" and gradually his wrath
subsided. Madame de Malivert had herself carried to her room, keeping
up admirably the pretence of a seizure. She sent to Paris for her own
Doctor.

The rest of the night passed charmingly. The gaiety of this happy
mother infected Octave and his mistress. Led on by Madame de
Malivert's merry speeches, Armance, who was still greatly upset and
had lost all self-control, ventured to let Octave see how dear he was
to her. She had the intense pleasure of seeing him jealous of the
Chevalier de Bonnivet. It was this fortunate sentiment which accounted
in a manner so gratifying to her for his apparent indifference during
the last few days. Mesdames d'Aumale and de Bonnivet, who had been
awakened in spite of Madame de Malivert's orders to the contrary, did
not appear until the night was far spent, and the whole party retired
to bed as dawn was breaking.

CHAPTER TWENTY-EIGHT

_This is the state of man: to-day he puts forth
The tender leaves of hope; to-morrow blossoms,
And bears his blushing honours thick upon him;
The third day comes a frost, a killing frost; ...
And then he falls--see his character.
KING HENRY VIII, Act III.
[Footnote: The last three words are added by Beyle. The source is
cited in all the editions as King Henry III.--C. K. S. M.]
Early on the following morning Madame de Malivert proceeded to Paris
to lay the plan of Octave's marriage before her husband. All day long
he held out against it; "not that you are to suppose," said the
Marquis, "that I have not long been expecting this stupid proposal. I
cannot pretend to be surprised. Mademoiselle de Zohiloff is not
absolutely penniless, I agree; her Russian uncles have died at a very
opportune moment for her. But her fortune is no greater than what we
might find elsewhere, and--what is of the greatest importance to my
son--there is no family connexion in this alliance; I can see nothing
m it but a deplorable similarity of character. Octave has not enough
relatives in society, and his reserved manner makes him no friends. He
will be a Peer when his cousin and I are gone, that is all, and, as
you know very well, my dear, in France, the value of a title depends
on the man who bears it. I belong to the older generation, as these
insolent fellows say; I shall soon pass away, and with me all the ties
that can connect my son with society; for he is an instrument in the
hands of our dear Marquise de Bonnivet, rather than an object of her
pursuit. We ought, in seeking a wife for Octave, to put social support
above fortune even. I grant him, if you like, the sort of exceptional
merit which succeeds by itself. I have always observed that these
sublime beings require to have their virtues preached, and my son, so
far from flattering the people who make or mar reputations, seems to
take a malicious pleasure in defying them to their faces. That is not
the way to achieve success. With a numerous connexion, well
established, he would have passed in society as a worthy candidate for
ministerial office; he has no one to sing his praises, he will be
regarded as merely an original."
Madame de Malivert protested volubly against this expression. She
could see that some one had been _buttonholing_ her husband.

His eloquence increased: "Yes, my dear, I would not swear that the readiness to take offence which Octave shews, and his passion for what are called _principles_, now that the Jacobins have changed all our customs including our language, may not lead him one day into the worst excess of folly, into what you call the _opposition_. The one outstanding man whom your opposition could boast, the Comte de Mirabeau, ended by selling himself; that is an ugly ending, and one that I should not care to see my son make." "Nor need you have any fear of his doing so," Madame de Malivert parried him boldly. "No, it is over the other precipice that my son's fortunes will be engulfed. This marriage will only make him a bumpkin, buried in the heart of the country, within the four walls of his manor. His sombre nature makes him too much inclined as it is to that sort of life. Our dear Armance has an odd way of looking at things; so far from attempting to alter what I find reprehensible in Octave, she will encourage him in his plebeian habits, and by this marriage you will destroy our family." "Octave will one day be summoned to the House of Peers, he will be a noble representative of the youth of France, and will win personal consideration by his eloquence." "There is too much competition. All these young Peers lay claim to eloquence. Why, good lord, they will be in their Chamber what they are in society, perfectly well mannered, highly educated, and that is all. All these young representatives of the youth of France will be the most bitter enemies of Octave, who has at least a point of view of his own."

Madame de Malivert returned late in the day to Andilly, with a charming letter for Armance, in which M. de Malivert besought her hand for his son.

Tired as she was by the exertions of the day, Madame de Malivert hastened to find Madame de Bonnivet, who must learn of the marriage from her lips alone. She let her see M. de Malivert's letter to Armance; she was only too glad to take this precaution against the people who might make her husband change his mind. This action was, moreover, necessary, the Marquise being in a sense Armance's guardian. This position sealed her lips. Madame de Malivert was grateful for the affection which Madame de Bonnivet shewed for Octave without at all seeming to approve personally of the marriage. The Marquise took refuge in enthusiastic praise of Mademoiselle de Zohiloff's character. Madame de Malivert did not forget to mention the overtures that she had made to Armance some months earlier, and the noble refusal made by the young orphan, who was then still penniless.

"Ah, it is not about Armance's noble qualities that my affection for Octave needs to be reassured," said the Marquise. "Any that she may have come from us. These family marriages are suitable only among the rich and powerful bankers; as their principal object is money, they are certain of finding it without trouble."

"We are coming to a time," replied Madame de Malivert, "when favour at Court, unless he chooses to purchase it by incessant personal services, will be merely a secondary object for a man of high birth, a Peer of France with a great fortune. Look at our friend Lord N------; his immense influence in his own country springs from the fact that he nominates eleven Members of the House of Commons. He never even sees his King."

It was in similar terms that Madame de Malivert met the objections raised by her brother, whose opposition was far stronger. Furious at the last night's scene and fully determined not to let the opportunity pass of making a great show of indignation, he wished, when he should allow his wrath to be appeased, to place his nephew under a burden of undying gratitude.

Octave, by himself, he would have forgiven, for after all he must either forgive him or abandon those dreams of wealth which had been occupying his thoughts, to the exclusion of all else, for the last year. As for the midnight scene, his vanity would have had the consolation, among his intimate friends, of Octave's well-known mania for throwing his mother's footmen out of windows.

But the thought of Armance reigning with absolute power over the heart of a husband who loved her to madness drove M. de Soubirane to declare that never again would he shew his face at Andilly. They were all very happy at Andilly, they took him more or less at his word, and, after offering him all sorts of apologies and invitations, proceeded to forget him.

Since he had seen his position strengthened by the arrival of the Chevalier de Bonnivet, who furnished him with good arguments and, at a pinch, with ready-made phrases, his antipathy towards Mademoiselle de Zo-hiloff had turned to hatred. He could not forgive her allusions to Russian bravery as displayed beneath the walls of Ismailoff, while the Knights of Malta, _sworn_ enemies of the Turks, sat idly upon their rock. The Commander might have forgotten an epigram provoked by himself; but the fact is that there was money at the bottom of all this anger with Armance. The Commander's head, never at any time too strong, was absolutely turned by the idea of making a vast fortune on

'Change. As is universal among commonplace natures, about the age of
fifty, the interest that he used to take in the things of this world
had died away, and boredom had made its appearance; as might also be
expected, the Commander had aspired successively to be a man of
letters, a political intriguer and a patron of the Italian opera. Only
some mischance had prevented his being a lay Jesuit.
Finally, the sport of gambling on 'Change haa appeared and had proved
a sovereign remedy for a vast boredom. And to gamble on 'Change he had
all the requirements save only funds and credit. The indemnity had
turned up at a most opportune moment, and the Commander had vowed that
he would have no difficulty in controlling his nephew, who was a mere
philosopher. He fully intended to invest on 'Change a good share of
the sum that Octave would receive from his mother's indemnity.
At the height of his passion for millions, Armance had presented
herself as an insuperable obstacle in the Commander's path. Now her
adoption into the family destroyed forever his hold over his nephew
and with it all his castles in the air crumbled. The Commander did not
waste any time in Paris, but went about fulminating against his
nephew's marriage in the houses of Madame la Duchesse de C------, the
head of the family, Madame la Duchesse d'Ancre, Madame de la Ronze,
Madame de Claix, whom he visited daily. All these friends of the
family soon decided that the marriage was most unsuitable.
In less than a week the young Vicomte's intended marriage was common
knowledge and was no less commonly deplored. The great ladies who had
marriageable daughters were furious.
"Madame de Malivert," said the Comtesse de Claix, "has the cruelty to
force that poor Octave into marrying her companion, evidently to save
the salary she would have to pay the girl; it's a shame."
In the midst of all this the Commander felt that he was forgotten in
Paris, where he was bored to death. The general outcry against
Octave's marriage could be no more permanent than anything else. He
must take advantage of this universal storm while it still lasted. A
marriage once arranged can be broken off only by prompt action.
Finally all these sound arguments and, more than they, his own boredom
brought it to pass that one fine morning the Commander was seen to
arrive at Andilly, where he resumed his old room and his ordinary life
as though nothing had occurred.
Every one was most polite to the newcomer, who did not fail to make
the most cordial overtures to his niece to be. "Friendship has its
illusions no less than love," he said to Armance, "and if I found

fault at first with certain proposals, it was because I too am passionately devoted to Octave."

CHAPTER TWENTY-NINE

Ses maux les plus cruels sont ceux qu'il se fait lui-même.
  BALZAC.

[Footnote: This quotation is presumably from the seventeenth century
letter writer, Guez de Balzac, whom Beyle in _Henri Brulard_ compares
with Chateaubriand.---C. K. R. M.]

Armance might perhaps have been taken in by these polite overtures,
but she did not stop to think about the Commander; she had other
grounds for anxiety.

Now that there was no longer any obstacle in the way of his marriage,
Octave was given to fits of sombre ill-temper which he found
difficulty in concealing; he pleaded a series of violent headaches,
and would go out riding by himself in the woods of Ecoucn and Senlis.
He would sometimes cover seven or eight leagues at a gallop. These
symptoms appeared ominous to Armance; she remarked that at certain
moments he gazed at her with eyes in which suspicion was more evident
than love.

It was true that these fits of sombre ill-temper ended as often as not
in transports of love and in a passionate abandonment which she had
never observed in him _in the days of their happiness_. It was thus
that she was beginning to describe, in her letters to Méry de Tersan,
the time that had passed between Octave's injury and her own fatal act
of imprudence in hiding in the closet by the Commander's room.
Since the announcement of her marriage, Armance had had the
consolation of being able to open her heart to her dearest friend.
Méry, brought up in a far from united family which was always being
torn asunder by fresh intrigues, was quite capable of giving her sound
advice.

During one of these long walks which she took with Octave in the
garden of the mansion, beneath Madame de Malivert's windows, Armance
said to him one day: "There is something so extraordinary in your
sadness that I, who love you and you alone in the world, have found it
necessary to seek the advice of a friend before venturing to speak to
you as I am going now to speak. You were happier before that cruel
night when I was so imprudent, and I have no need to tell you that all
my own happiness has vanished far more rapidly than yours. I have a
suggestion to make to you: let us return to a state of perfect
happiness and to that pleasant intimacy which was the delight of my

life, after I knew that you loved me, until that fatal idea arose of
our marriage. I shall take upon myself entire responsibility for so
odd a change. I shall tell people that I have made a vow never to
marry. They will condemn the idea, it will impair the good opinion
that some of my friends are kind enough to hold of me; what do I care?
Public opinion is after all important to a girl with money only so
long as she thinks of marry ing; and I certainly shall never marry."
Octave's only answer was to take her hand, while tears streamed from
his eyes in abundance. "Oh, my dear angel," he said to her, "how far
superior you are to me!" The sight of these tears on the face of a man
not ordinarily subject to that weakness combined with so simple a
speech to destroy all Armance's resolution.
At length she said to him with an effort: "Answer me, my friend.
Accept a proposal which is going to restore my happiness. We shall
continue to spend our time together just as much as before." She saw a
servant approaching them. "The luncheon bell is going to ring," she
went on in some distress, "your father will be arriving from Paris,
afterwards I shall not have another opportunity of speaking to you,
and if I do not speak to you I shall be unhappy and agitated all day,
for I shall be a little doubtful of you." "You! Doubtful of me!" said
Octave gazing at her in a way which for a moment banished all her
fears.
After walking for some minutes in silence: "No, Octave," Armance went
on, "I am not doubtful of you; if I doubted your love, I hope that God
would grant me the blessing of death; but after all you have been less
happy since your marriage was settled." "I shall talk to you as I
should to myself," said Octave impetuously. "There are moments in
which I am far more happy, for now at last I have the certainty that
nothing in the world can separate me from you; I shall be able to see
you and to talk to you at every hour of the day, _but_," he went on...
and fell into one of those moods of gloomy silence which filled
Armance with despair.
The dread of hearing the luncheon bell, which was going to separate
them for the rest of the day perhaps, gave her for the second time the
courage to break in upon Octave's musings: "But what, dear?" she asked
him, "tell me all; that fearful _but_ is making me a hundred times
more wretched than anything you could add to it."
"Very well!" said Octave stopping short, turning to face her and
gazing fixedly at her, no longer with the gaze of a lover but so as to
be able to read her thoughts, "you shall know all; death itself would

be less painful to me than the story which I have to tell you, but also I love you far more than life. Do I need to swear to you, no longer as your lover" (and at that moment his eyes were indeed no longer the eyes of a lover) "but as an honourable man and as I should swear to your father, if heaven in its mercy had spared him to us, do I need to swear to you that I love you and you only in the world, as I have never loved before and shall never love again? To be parted from you would be death to me and a hundred times worse than death; but I have a fearful secret which I have never confided to any one, this secret will explain to you my fatal vagaries."

As he stammered rather than spoke these words, Octave's features contracted, there was a hint of madness in his eyes; one would have said he no longer saw Armance; his lips twitched convulsively. Armance, more wretched than he, leaned upon the tub of an orange tree; she shuddered on recognising that fatal orange tree by which she had fainted when Octave spoke harshly to her after the night he had spent in the forest. Octave had stopped and stood facing her as though horror-stricken and not daring to continue. His startled eyes gazed fixedly in front of him as though he beheld a vision of a monster.

"Dear friend," said Armance, "I was more unhappy when you spoke cruelly to me by this same orange tree months ago; at that time I doubted your love. What am I saying?" she corrected herself with passion. "On that fatal day I was certain that you did not love me. Ah! my friend, how far happier I am to-day!"

The accent of truth with which Armance uttered these last words seemed to moderate the bitter, angry grief to which Octave was a prey. Armance, forgetful of her customary reserve, clasped his hand passionately and urged him to speak; her face came for a moment so close to his that he could feel her warm breath. This sensation moved him to tenderness; speech became easy to him.

"Yes, dear friend," he said to her, gazing at length into her eyes, "I adore you, you need not doubt my love; but what is the man who adores you? He is a _monster_."

With these words, Octave's tenderness seemed to forsake him; all at once he flew into a fury, tore himself irom the arms of Armance who tried in vain to hold him back, and took to his heels. Armance remained motionless. At that instant the bell rang for luncheon. More dead than alive, she had only to shew her face before Madame de Malivert to obtain leave not to remain at table. Octave's servant came in a moment later to say that a sudden engagement had obliged his master to set off at a gallop for Paris.

The party at luncheon was silent and chilly; the only happy person was the Commander. Struck by this simultaneous absence of both the young people, he detected tears of anxiety in his sister's eyes; he felt a momentary joy. It seemed to him that the affair of the marriage was no longer going quite so well: "marriages have been broken off later than this," he said to himself, and the intensity of his preoccupation prevented him from making himself agreeable to Mesdames d'Aumale and de Bonnivet. The arrival of the Marquis, who had come from Paris, notwithstanding a threatening of gout, and shewed great annoyance at not finding Octave whom he had warned of his coming, increased the Commander's joy. "The moment is auspicious," he told himself, "for making the voice of reason heard." As soon as luncheon was over, Mesdames d'Aumale and de Bonnivet went upstairs to their rooms; Madame de Malivert disappeared into Armance's room, and the Commander was animated, that is to say happy, for an hour and a quarter, which he employed in trying to shake his brother-in-law's determination in the matter of Octave's marriage.

There was a strong vein of honesty underlying everything that the old Marquis said in reply. "The indemnity belongs to your sister," he said; "I myself am a pauper. It is this indemnity which makes it possible for us to think of establishing Octave in life; your sister is more anxious than he, I think, for this marriage with Armance, who, for that matter, has some fortune of her own; in all this I can do nothing, as a man of honour, but express my opinion; it would be impossible for me to speak with authority; I should have the air of wishing to deprive my wife of the pleasure of spending the rest of her life with her dearest friend."

Madame de Malivert had found Armance greatly agitated but scarcely communicative. Urged by the call of affection, Armance spoke in the vaguest terms of a trifling quarrel, such as occurs at times between people who are most fervently in love. "I am sure that Octave is to blame," said Madame de Malivert as she rose to go, "otherwise you would tell me all;" and she left Armance to herself. This was doing her a great service. It soon became plain to her that Octave had committed some serious crime, the dread consequences of which he might perhaps have exaggerated, and that as a man of honour he would not allow her to unite her destiny with that of one who was perhaps a murderer, without letting her know the whole truth.

Dare we say that this explanation of Octave's eccentricity restored his cousin to a sort of tranquillity? She went down to the garden, half hoping to find him there. She felt herself at that moment entirely rid of the profound jealousy which Madame d'Aumale had inspired in her; she did not, it is true, admit to herself that this might account for the state of blissful emotion in which she found herself. She felt herself transported by the most tender and most generous pity.

"If we have to leave France," she said to herself, "and go into banishment far away, were it even in America, well, away we shall go," she said to herself with joy, "and the sooner the better." And her imagination began to wander, picturing a life of complete solitude on a desert island, ideas too romantic and, what is more, too familiar on the pages of novels to be recorded here. Neither on that day nor on the next did Octave put in an appearance: only on the evening of the second day Armance received a letter dated from Paris. Never had she been so happy. The most burning, the most abandoned passion glowed in this letter. "Ah! If he had been here at the moment when he wrote, he would have told me all." Octave let it be understood that he was detained in Paris because he was ashamed to tell her his secret. "It is not at every moment," the letter went on, "that I shall have the courage to utter that fatal word, even to you, for it may destroy the sentiments which you deign to feel for me and which are everything to me. Do not press me upon this subject, dear friend." Armance made haste to reply to him by a servant who was waiting. "Your greatest crime," she told him, "is your remaining away from us," and she was no less surprised than joyful when, half an hour after writing to him, she saw Octave appear, he having come out to await her answer at Labarre near Andilly.

The days that followed were days of unbroken happiness. The illusions induced by the passion that was animating Armance were so strange that presently she found herself quite accustomed to the idea of being in love with a murderer. It seemed to her that it must at the very least be murder, this crime of which Octave hesitated to admit himself guilty. Her cousin spoke too carefully to exaggerate his ideas, and he had used these very words: "I am a monster."

In the first love letter that she had ever written to him or to any one, she had promised him that she would not ask him questions; this vow was sacred in her eyes. Octave's letter to her in reply she treasured. She had read it a score of times, she formed the habit of writing every evening to the man who was to be her husband; and as it would have made her blush to speak his name to her maid, she concealed her first letter in the tub of that orange tree which Octave had good reason to know.

She informed him of this in a word one morning as they were sitting down to luncheon. He left the room with the excuse that he had to give an order, and Armance had the indescribable pleasure, when he returned a quarter of an hour later, of reading in his eyes the expression of the keenest happiness and tenderest gratitude.

A day or two after this, Armance found the courage to write to him: "I believe you to be guilty of some great crime; it shall be our lifelong duty to atone for it, if atonement be possible; but the strange thing is that I am perhaps even more tenderly devoted to you than before this confidence.

"I feel how much this avowal must have cost you, it is the first great sacrifice that you have ever made for me, and, let me tell you, it is only from that moment that I have been cured of an ugly sentiment which I too scarcely dared confess to you. I imagine the worst. And so it seems to me that you need not make me a more detailed confession before a certain ceremony is performed. You will not have deceived me, I swear to you. God pardons the penitent, and I am sure that you are exaggerating your offence; were it as grave as it can be, I, who have seen your anxieties, forgive you. You will make me a full confession in a year from now, perhaps you will then be less afraid of me.... I cannot, however, promise to love you more dearly."

A number of letters written in this strain of angelic goodness had almost made Octave decide to confide in writing to his mistress the secret that she was entitled to learn; but the shame, the embarrassment of writing such a letter still held him back.

He went to Paris to consult M. Dolier, the relative who had acted as his second. He knew that M. Dolier was a man of honour, endowed with a straightforward mind and not clever enough to compound with his duty or to indulge in illusions. Octave asked him whether he was absolutely bound to confide in Mademoiselle de Zohiloff a fatal secret, which he would not have hesitated to disclose, before his marriage, to her father or guardian. He went so far as to shew M. Dolier the part of Armance's letter which we have quoted above.

"You can have no excuse for not speaking," was the gallant officer's reply, "it is your bounden duty. You must not take advantage of Mademoiselle de Zohiloff's generosity. It would be unworthy of you to deceive any one, and it would be even more beneath the noble Octave to deceive a poor orphan who has perhaps no friend but himself among all the men of her family."

Octave had told himself all this a thousand times, but it acquired an entirely new force when it issued from the lips of a firm and honourable man.

Octave thought he heard the voice of destiny speaking.

He took his leave of M. Dolier vowing that he would write the fatal letter in the first café that he should find on his right hand after leaving his cousin's house; he kept his word. He wrote a letter of ten lines and addressed it to Mademoiselle de Zohiloff, at the Château de-------, by Andilly.

On leaving the café, he looked about him for a letterbox; as luck would have it, there was none to be seen. Presently a remnant of that awkward feeling which urged him to postpone such a confession as long as Possible, succeeded in persuading him that a letter of such importance ought not to be entrusted to the post, that it was better that he should place it himself in the tub of the orange tree in the garden at Andilly. Octave had not the intelligence to see in the idea of this postponement a lingering illusion of a passion that was barely conquered.

The essential thing, in his situation, was for him not to give way an inch to the repugnance which M. Dolier's stern advice had helped him to overcome. He mounted his horse to carry his letter to Andilly.

Since the morning on which the Commander had had a suspicion of some misunderstanding between the lovers, the natural frivolity of his character had given way to an almost incessant desire to do them an injury.

He had taken as confidant the Chevalier de Bonnivet. All the time that the Commander had formerly employed in dreaming of speculations on 'Change and in jotting down figures in a pocket-book, he now devoted to seeking a way in which to break off his nephew's engagement.

His proposals at first were none too reasonable; the Chevalier de Bonnivet regularised his plan of attack. He suggested to him that he should have Armance followed, and, by spending a few louis, the Commander made spies of all the servants in the house. They told him that Octave and Armance were corresponding, and that they concealed their letters in the tub of an orange tree bearing a certain number. Such imprudence appeared incredible to the Chevalier de Bonnivet. He left the Commander to think over it. Seeing at the end of a week that

M. de Soubirane had progressed farther than the obvious idea of reading the amorous expressions of a pair of lovers, he skilfully reminded him that, among a score of different foibles, he had had, for six months, a passion for autograph letters; the Commander had employed at that time a very clever copyist. This idea penetrated that thick skull but produced no effect. It had the company there, however, of a burning hatred.

The Chevalier hesitated long before risking himself with such a man. The sterility of his associate's mind was discouraging. Moreover, at the first check, he might confess everything. Fortunately, the Chevalier remembered a vulgar novel in which the villain has the lovers' handwriting copied and fabricates forged letters. The Commander read scarcely anything, but had at one time worshipped fine bindings. The Chevalier decided to make a final attempt; should this prove unsuccessful, he would abandon the Commander to all the aridity of his own methods. One of Thouvenin's men, lavishly paid, worked day and night and clothed in a superb binding the novel in which the trick of forging letters occurred. The Chevalier took this sumptuous book, brought it out to Andilly and stained with coffee the page on which the substitution of the forged letters was described.

"I am in despair," he said one morning to the Commander as he entered his room. "Madame de-------, who is mad about her books, as you know, has had this miserable novel bound in the most beautiful style. I was ass enough to pick it up in her house, and have stained one of the pages. Now you have collected or invented the most astounding secrets for doing everything, could not you shew me how to forge a new page?" The Chevalier, having discoursed at great length and used the expressions most akin to the idea that he wished to suggest, left the volume in the Commander's room.

He mentioned it to him at least ten times before it occurred to M. de Soubirane to hatch a quarrel between the lovers by means of forged letters.

He was so proud of this idea that at first he was inclined to exaggerate its importance; he spoke of it in this light to the Chevalier, who was horrified at so immoral an action and left that evening for Paris. A couple of days later the Commander, in the course of conversation with him, returned to his idea. "To substitute a forged letter would be atrocious," cried the Chevalier. "Is your love for your nephew so strong that _the end justifies the means_?" But the reader is doubtless no less tired than ourselves of these sordid details; details in which we see the cankered fruit of the new generation competing with the frivolity of the old.

The Commander, still full of pity for the Chevalier's innocence, proved to him that, in an almost hopeless cause, the most certain way to be defeated was to attempt nothing.

M. de Soubirane boldly rescued from his sister's hearth a number of scraps of Armance's handwriting, and easily obtained from his penman copies which it was hard to distinguish from their originals. He had already begun to base his hopes of a breach of Octave's engagement upon the most definite anticipations of the intrigues of the coming winter, the distractions of the ballroom, the advantageous offers which he would be able to have made to the family. The Chevalier de Bonnivet was filled with admiration for his character. "Why is not this man a Minister," he said to himself, "the highest offices would be mine. But with this cursed Charter, public debates, the liberty of the press, never could such a man become a Minister, however noble his birth." Finally, after he had waited patiently for a fortnight, it occurred to the Commander to compose a letter from Armance to Méry de Tersan, her dearest friend. The Chevalier was for the second time on the point of throwing up the sponge. M. de Soubirane had spent two days in drafting a model letter sparkling with wit and overloaded with delicate fancies, a reminiscence of the letters he himself used to write in 1789.

"Our generation is more serious than that," the Chevalier told him, "you should aim at being pedantic, grave, boring.... Your letter is charming; the Chevalier de Laclos would not have disowned it, but it will not take in any one to-day." "Always to-day, today!" retorted the Commander, "your Laclos was nothing but a fool. I do not know why all you young men model yourselves on him. His characters drivel like barbers," etc., etc.

The Chevalier was enchanted with the Commander's hatred for Laclos; he put up a stout defence of the author of _Les liaisons dangereuses_, was completely routed, and finally obtained a model letter, not nearly emphatic or German enough for his purpose, but still quite reasonable. The model letter drafted after so stormy a discussion was presented by the Commander to his copier of autographs who, thinking that it was merely a question of epistolary gallantry, raised only the objections necessary to secure ample payment for himself, and produced a lifelike imitation of Mademoiselle de Zohiloff's hand. Armance was supposed to be writing her friend Méry de Tersan a long letter about her approaching marriage to Octave.

As he returned to Andilly with the letter written according to M. Dolier's suggestions, the predominant thought in Octave's mind throughout his ride had been that he must make Armance promise not to read his letter until they had parted for the night. Octave intended to leave the following morning at daybreak; he was quite certain that Armance would write in reply. He hoped thus somewhat to diminish the awkwardness of a first meeting after such a confession. He had made up his mind to this course only because he discerned an element of heroism in Armance's attitude. For a long time past he had never surprised her at any moment in her life when she was not dominated by the happiness or grief arising from the sentiment that united them. Octave had no doubt that she felt a violent passion for himself. Arriving at Andilly he sprang from the saddle, ran to the garden and there, as he was hiding his letter beneath some leaves in the corner of the orange-tree tub, found one from Armance.

CHAPTER THIRTY

He withdrew rapidly to the shelter of a lime alley to be able to read
it without interruption. He saw from the opening lines that this
letter was intended for Mademoiselle Méry de Tersan (it was the letter
composed by the Commander). But the opening lines had so disturbed
him that he went on, and read: "I do not know how to reply to your
reproaches. You are right, my kind friend, I am mad to complain. This
arrangement is, from every point of view, far better than anything a
poor girl, who has woken up to find herself rich, and has no family to
establish and protect her, could expect. He is a man of parts and of
the highest virtue: perhaps he has too much virtue for me. Shall I
confess it to you? The times have indeed changed; what would have
been the height of bliss for me a few months ago is no more now than a
duty; has heaven withheld from me the power to love constantly? I am
completing an arrangement that is reasonable and advantageous, as I
repeat to myself incessantly, but my heart no longer knows those sweet
transports that I used to feel at the sight of the most perfect man,
in my eyes, to be found anywhere upon earth, the one being worthy to
be loved. I see to-day that his mood is inconstant, or rather why
accuse him? It is not he that has changed; my whole misfortune is that
there is inconstancy in my heart. I am about to contract a marriage
that is advantageous, honourable, in every sense; but, dear Méry, I
blush to confess it to you; I am no longer marrying the person whom I
loved above all; I find him serious and at times barely entertaining,
and it is with him that I am going to spend my life! Probably in some
lonely manor house in the depths of the country where we shall promote
the spread of pupil-teaching and vaccination. Perhaps, dear friend, I
shall look back with regret upon Madame de Bonnivet's drawing-room;
who would have said so six months ago? This strange fickleness in my
character is what distresses me most. Is not Octave the most
remarkable young man we have seen this winter? But I have had so
miserable a girlhood! I should like an amusing husband. Farewell.
The day after to-morrow _I am to be allowed_ to go to Paris; at eleven
I shall be at your door."
Octave stood horror-stricken. All at once he awoke as though from a
dream and ran to retrieve the letter which he had just left in the tub
of the orange tree: he tore it up furiously, and put the fragments in
his pocket.

"I needed," he said to himself coldly, "the wildest and profoundest passion if I was to be pardoned for my fatal secret. In defiance of all reason, in defiance of every vow I had made to myself throughout my life, I thought I had met with a creature above the rest of humanity. To deserve such an exception, I should have had to be pleasant and gay, and those are the qualities that I lack. I have been mistaken; there is nothing left for me but to die.

"It would doubtless be an offence against the laws of honour not to make a confession, were I involving for all time the destiny of Mademoiselle de Zohiloff. But I can leave her free within a month. She will be a young widow, rich, very beautiful, no doubt greatly sought after; and the name of Malivert will be of greater use to her in finding an _amusing husband_ than the still unfamiliar name of Zohiloff."

It was in this frame of mind that Octave entered his mother's room, where he found Armance who was talking of him and longing for his return; soon she was as pale and almost as unhappy as himself, and yet he had just said to his mother that he could not endure the delays that kept postponing the date of his marriage. "There are plenty of people who would be glad to mar my happiness," he had gone on to say; "I am certain of it. Why do we need all these preparations? Armance is richer than I am, and it is not likely that she will ever want for clothes or jewels. I venture to hope that before the end of the second year of our marriage she will be gay, happy, enjoying all the pleasures of Paris, and that she will never repent of the step she is now about to take. I am sure that she will never be buried in the country in an old manor house."

There was something so strange in the sound of Octave's words, so little in keeping with the aspiration that they expressed, that almost simultaneously Armance and Madame de Malivert felt their eyes fill with tears. Armance could barely find strength to reply: "Ah, dear friend, how cruel you are!"

Greatly vexed that he had not managed to assume an air of happiness, Octave left the room abruptly. His determination to end his marriage by death imparted a certain harshness and cruelty to his manner. Having deplored with Armance what she called her son's madness, Madame de Malivert came to the conclusion that solitude was of no avail'to a character that was naturally sombre. "Do you love him still in spite of this defect from which he is the first to suffer?" said Madame de Malivert; "consult your heart, my child, I have no wish to make you unhappy, everything may yet be broken off." "Oh, Mama, I believe that I love him even more than ever, now that I no longer think him so perfect." "Very well, my pet," replied Madame de Malivert, "I shall have you married in a week from now. Until then, be indulgent to him, he loves you, you cannot doubt that. You know what he feels about his duty to his family, and yet you saw his fury when he thought you were being made the butt of my brother's wicked tongue. Be kind and good, my dear child, with this creature who is being made wretched by some odd prejudice against marriage." Armance, to whom these words spoken at random presented so true a meaning, increased her attentions and tender devotion to Octave.

The following day, at dawn, Octave came to Paris, and spent a very considerable sum, almost two-thirds of what he had at his disposal, in buying costly jewelry which he included among the wedding presents. He called upon his father's lawyer and made him insert in the marriage contract certain clauses extremely advantageous to the bride to be, which, in the event of her widowhood, assured her the most ample independence.

It was with business of this sort that Octave occupied the ten days that elapsed between the discovery of Armance's supposed letter and his marriage. These days were for Octave more tranquil than he could have dared to hope. What makes misery so cruel to tender hearts is a little ray of hope which sometimes lingers.

Octave had no hope. His course was decided, and for a stout heart, however hard the part he may have to play, it dispenses him from reflecting upon his fate, and asks no more of him than the courage to perform it scrupulously; which is a small matter.

What most impressed Octave, when the necessary preparations and business of all sorts left him to himself, was a prolonged astonishment: What! So Mademoiselle de Zohiloflf no longer meant anything to him! He was so far accustomed to believe firmly in the eternity of his love and of their intimate relation, that at every moment he kept forgetting that all was changed, he was incapable of imagining life without Armance. Almost every morning, he was obliged when he awoke to remind himself of his misery. It was a cruel moment. But presently the thought of death came to console him and to restore calm to his heart. At the same time, towards the end of this interval of ten days, Armance's extreme tenderness caused him some moments of weakness. During their solitary walks, thinking herself authorised by the imminence of their marriage, Armance allowed herself on more than one occasion to take Octave's hand, which was beautifully shaped, and to raise it to her lips. This increase of tender attentions of which Octave was quite well aware, and, in spite of himself, extremely sensible, often made keen and poignant a grief which he believed himself to have overcome.

He pictured to himself what those caresses would have been coming from a person who really loved him, coining from Armance as, on her own admission, in the fatal letter to Méry, she had still been two months since. "And my want of friendliness and gaiety has been able to kill her love," said Octave bitterly to himself. "Alas! It was the art of making myself welcome in society that I ought to have studied instead of abandoning myself to all those useless sciences! What good have they done me? What good have I had from my success with Madame d'Aumale? She would have loved me had I wished it. I was not made to please those whom I respect. Evidently a wretched shyness makes me sad, wanting in friendliness, just when I am passionately anxious to please.

"Armance has always alarmed me. I have never approached her without feeling that I was appearing before the ruler of my destiny. I ought to have derived from my experience, and from what I could see going on round about me, a more accurate idea of the effect produced by a pleasant man who seeks to interest a girl of twenty....

"But all that is useless now," said Octave, breaking off with a melancholy sigh: "my life is ended. _Vixi et quem, dederat fortuna sortem peregi."

[Footnote: When dying, abandoned by Aeneas, Dido exclaims: "I have lived and have run the course which fortune appointed for me." [Octave shows a certain indifference here to the laws of prosody. Virgil's line (Aeneid IV, 653), runs: _Vixi et quem dederat cursum fortuna peregi_.--C. K. S. M.]

In certain moments of sombre humour, Octave went so far as to interpret Armance's tender manner, so little in keeping with the extreme reserve which was so natural to her, as the performance of a disagreeable duty which she had set herself. Nothing then could be comparable to his rudeness, which really had almost the appearance of insanity.

Less wretched at other moments, he allowed himself to be touched by the seductive grace of this girl who was to be his bride. It would indeed have been difficult to imagine anything more touching or more noble than the caressing ways of a girl who was ordinarily so reserved, doing violence to the habits of a lifetime in the attempt to restore a little calm to the man whom she loved. She believed him to be the victim of remorse and yet felt a violent passion for him. Now that the main occupation of Armance's life was no longer to conceal her love and to reproach herself for it, Octave had become dearer to her than ever.

One day, on a walk in the direction of the woods of Ecouen, carried away herself by the tender words which she was venturing to utter, Armance went so far as to say to him, and at the moment she meant what she was saying: "I sometimes think of committing a crime equal to yours so as to deserve that you shall no longer fear me." Octave, charmed by the accents of true passion, and understanding all that was in her mind, stopped short to gaze fixedly at her, and in another moment might have given her the letter containing his confession, the fragments of which he still carried on his person. As he thrust his hand into the pocket of his coat, he felt the finer paper of the false letter addressed to Méry de Tersan, and his good intention froze.

CHAPTER THIRTY-ONE

If he be turn'd to earth, let me but give him one hearty kiss,
and you shall put us both into one coffin.
WEBSTER.

[Footnote: From _Vittoria Corombona_, Act IV. Cornelia finds her son
Marcello killed by his brother Flamineo.--C. K. S. M.]

Octave was involved in endless conciliations of important relatives
whom he knew to disapprove strongly of his marriage. In ordinary
circumstances, nothing would have annoyed him more. He would have
come away wretched and almost disgusted with his prospective happiness
from the mansions of his illustrious kinsfolk. Greatly to his surprise
he found, as he performed these duties, that nothing caused him any
annoyance; because nothing now interested him any more. He was dead to
the world.

Since the revelation of Armance's fickleness, men were for him
creatures of an alien species. Nothing had power to move him, neither
the misfortunes of virtue nor the prosperity of crime. A secret voice
said to him: these wretches are less wretched than you.

Octave carried through with admirable indifference all the idiotic
formalities that modern civilisation has piled up to mar a happy day.
The marriage was celebrated.

Taking advantage of what is now becoming an established custom, Octave
set off at once with Armance for the domain of Malivert, situated in
Dauphiné; and in the end took her to Marseilles. There he informed her
that he had made a vow to go to Greece, where he would shew that,
notwithstanding his distaste for military ways, he knew how to wield a
sword. Armance had been so happy since her marriage that she consented
without undue regret to this temporary separation. Octave himself,
being unable to conceal from himself Armance's happiness, was guilty
of what was in his eyes the very great weakness of postponing his
departure for a week, which he spent in visiting with her the Holy
Balm, the Château Borelli and other places in the neighbourhood of
Marseilles. He was greatly touched by the happiness of his young
bride. "She is playing a part," he said to himself, "her letter to
Méry is a clear proof of it; but she plays it so well!" He underwent
moments of self-deception when Armance's perfect felicity succeeded in
making him happy. "What other woman in the world," Octave asked
himself, "even by the most sincere sentiments, could give me such

happiness?"

At length it was time for them to part; once on board the ship, Octave paid dearly for his moments of self-deception. For some days he could no longer summon up courage to die. "I should be the lowest of mankind," he said to himself, "and a coward in my own eyes, if after hearing my sentence uttered by the wise Dolier, I do not speedily give Armance back her freedom. I lose little by departing from this life," he added with a sigh; "if Armance plays the lover so gracefully, it is merely a reminiscence, she is recalling what she felt for me in the past. Before long I should have begun to bore her. She respects me, no doubt, but has no longer any passionate feeling for me, and my death will distress her without plunging her in despair." This painful certainty succeeded in making Octave forget the heavenly beauty of an Armance intoxicated with love, and swooning in his arms on the eve of his departure. He regained courage, and from the third day at sea, with his courage there reappeared tranquillity. The vessel happened to be passing the Island of Corsica. The memory of a great man who had died so pitiably occurred vividly to Octave and began to restore his firmness of purpose. As he thought of him incessantly, he almost had him as a witness to his conduct. He feigned a mortal malady. Fortunately, the only medical officer that they had on board was an old ship's carpenter who claimed to understand fever, and he was the first to be taken in by Octave's alarming state and by his ravings. By dint of playing his part for a few moments now and again, Octave saw at the end of a week that they despaired of his recovery. He sent for the captain in what was called one of his lucid intervals, and dictated his will, which was witnessed by the nine persons composing the crew.

Octave had taken care to deposit a similar will with a lawyer at Marseilles. He bequeathed everything that was at his disposal to his wife, on the strange condition that she should remarry within twenty months of his death. If Madame Octave de Malivert did not think fit to comply with this condition, he begged his mother to accept his fortune.

Having signed his testament in the presence of the entire crew, Octave sank into a state of extreme weakness and asked for the prayers for the dying, which several Italian sailors repeated by his bedside. He wrote to Armance, and enclosed in his letter the other which he had had the courage to write to her from a café in Paris, and the letter to her friend Méry de Tersan which he had intercepted in the tub of the orange tree. Never had Octave so fallen under the spell of the most tender love as at this supreme moment. Except for the nature of his death, he gave himself the happiness of telling Armance everything. Octave continued to languish for more than a week, every day he gave himself the fresh pleasure of writing to his beloved. He entrusted his letters to various sailors, who promised him that they would convey them in person to his lawyer at Marseilles.

A ship's boy, from the crow's nest, cried: "Land!" It was the shores of Greece and the mountains of the Morea that had come into sight on the horizon. A fresh breeze bore the vessel rapidly on. The name of Greece revived Octave's courage: "I salute thee," he murmured, "O land of heroes!" And at midnight, on the third of March, as the moon was rising behind Mount Kalos, a mixture of opium and digitalis prepared by himself delivered Octave peacefully from a life which had been so agitated. At break of day, they found him lying motionless on the bridge, leaning against a coil of rope. A smile was on his lips, and his rare beauty impressed even the sailors who gave him burial. The manner of his death was never suspected in France save by Armance alone. Shortly afterwards, the Marquis de Malivert having died, Armance and Madame de Malivert took the veil in the same convent.

Made in United States
Orlando, FL
01 June 2023